HOLY MATRIMONY

ANNABELLE MARIN

Published by Blushing Books
An Imprint of
ABCD Graphics and Design, Inc.
A Virginia Corporation
977 Seminole Trail #233
Charlottesville, VA 22901

Holy Matrimony
Annabelle Marin

EBook ISBN: 978-1-63954-436-3
Print ISBN: 978-1-63954-437-0

The Bennington Family Tree

Paul Bennington (1821-1870)
Petunia Bennington (1822-1859)
Christopher Bennington (b.1840. 30 years old)
Steve Bennington (b.1842. 28 years old)
Hugh Bennington (b.1845. 25 years old)
Poppy Bennington (b.1845. 25 years old)
Anthony Bennington (b.1849. 21 years old)
Iris Bennington (b.1855. 15 years old)
Lily Bennington (b.1859. 11 years old)

Chapter 1

LARKSPUR VALLEY, *Wyoming. February 1870.*

Christopher Bennington had often been accused of being a man who lacked sympathy. But he simply preferred to see it as someone who didn't waste tears or showcase grand displays of emotions on trivial things. At thirty years old there were, according to him, very few things in his life in which tears were an appropriate reaction as a grown man.

A broken bone. The loss of a wife. Illness.

But Christopher Bennington had never broken a bone, wasn't married, and he couldn't remember the last time he had been ill. He could remember the last time he had thought about crying when old Dr. Peterson had informed the rather large Bennington family that the matriarch, Mrs. Petunia Bennington, barely thirty-seven, had died giving birth to the seventh Bennington sibling. Baby Lily, Mrs. Bennington had named all her daughters after her favorite flowers, had come into the world screaming just as her mother had taken her last breath.

Mrs. Bennington had been ill during her entire pregnancy with Lily, but her brood had never thought she would actually die. Christopher had been just nineteen when she had died, practically a grown man who was being groomed to take over the Bennington's successful horse and cattle ranch his English great-grandfather had built from the ground up in 1800.

When Dr. Peterson had delivered the news gravely to the wide-eyed siblings and their grief-stricken father, he had allowed himself two tears to slip down his cheeks and then he stopped. For his siblings needed comfort especially Anthony and Iris who were practically babies at ten and four. And his father who looked ready to drown himself in a river even though he had seven children to take care of, one of them who was a newborn daughter.

So, Christopher Bennington didn't allow himself to cry even though he had just lost his sweet mother. The woman who always managed to make him smile, even when he was surly, and who caused joy by doing something as simple as singing a song. His siblings needed him. His father needed him. Christopher lived to serve, to feel useful.

"Are you paying attention?" Steve, the second oldest Bennington sibling, hissed at him. His shiny gold sheriff's badge caught his attention. The blue eyes all the Bennington siblings were blessed with were darting from Christopher to Pastor James who was performing the funeral services for their father.

Christopher threw Steve a dirty look as he looked, for what felt like the first time that morning, at the mourners who were accompanying them to say goodbye to the widower Paul Bennington. The majority of the town was there as the former patriarch had been jolly and a well-respected member of the community. His sudden death at forty-nine from a nasty rattlesnake bite had been a shock to say the least. It had been said the older man had been crawling, nearly dead, when two of his workers had found him. The upside, some of the townspeople whispered, was he was finally reunited with his beloved wife whom he married when the pair of them were in their late teens.

The eldest Bennington sibling's blue eyes first went to his fraternal twin siblings, twenty-five-year-old Hugh and Poppy nicknamed "Evil Twins" affectionally based on their prickly personalities. Hugh was in his last year of medical school at a private university, a two days' journey from Larkspur Valley. Hugh had dark hair and icy blue eyes which he used to glance coldly at the crowd. Once or twice the Bennington siblings had teased him about whether or not he had an actual soul or if he was Lucifer reincarnated.

Next to him stood his twin sister, Poppy Bennington, her hair a buttery yellow instead of onyx black. Poppy had taken over the motherly role at just fourteen-years-old when their mother had passed, and while she was revered as a goddess by Anthony, Iris, and Lily whom she had practically raised, her elder brothers worried her horrid temper would land her in hot water sooner or later. Even Christopher had lost control of her and, feeling inept when it came to childrearing, their father had practically let Poppy get away with murder.

Next to Poppy stood Finn Weston, Christopher's right-hand man. He was dressed in his Sunday best suit looking at Christopher's blonde sister with big cow eyes. He was only two years older than Poppy and had fallen in love with her from the first second he saw her. Unfortunately for him, Poppy could be a little hellion and had refused his advances even though she was past marriable age. Her last beau had broken her heart when he moved back to Massachusetts two years ago.

Twenty-one-year-old Anthony Bennington stood across

from Poppy looking overly thin and lanky. Christopher made a mental note to ask him if he was all right, he had always been the most sensitive out of the four boys and he worried he spent too much time alone. He was in his third year of divinity school studying to be a pastor in Laramie, Wyoming.

Their sister, fifteen-year-old Iris, was holding his hand tightly while whispering comforting words in his ear. She was still a schoolgirl, but in some ways more mature and kind-hearted than Poppy who had been forced to grow up at a young age. She had it in her head that she was going to be a schoolteacher even though none of her brothers were fond of the idea of Iris working.

The youngest Bennington sibling, eleven-year-old Lily, was sobbing into her hankie wearing a too tight black dress which had been dyed black at the last minute because she didn't have any mourning clothes. Poor Lily had lost both parents by age eleven.

Even though Pastor James was still finishing his prayer all six siblings were staring at Christopher waiting for his next move. His skin prickled as he realized he was now the head of the Bennington household, the person who was going to be responsible for all his siblings and their futures even though Lily and Iris were the only ones not of age. They were going to be looking up to him for advice and guidance not his father who was six feet underground. The idea fright-ened him even though he would never admit it out loud, not even to Steve and definitely not to Hugh.

Pastor James finally closed his Bible as he looked at the Bennington family. "May our brother Paul Bennington rest in peace and may our Lord and savior give strength and guidance to his family. Amen."

The rest of the afternoon went in a blur: flowers thrown over his recently buried father's casket, accepting the condo-lences from townspeople, Poppy and Iris running around giving guests lemonade and a piece of Bundt cake, Christopher consoling a hysterical Lily when she threw a tantrum. By the time six o'clock in the evening rolled around Christopher was exhausted and could barely finish the dinner Poppy had served him.

He glanced wearily at Hugh and Anthony who had very different expressions on their faces. Anthony looked like he was going to be sick, and Hugh was smoking in the house in front of the younger girls which made Christopher want to smack him. Thankfully, Steve took care of that for him.

"When are you two heading back to school?"

"Saturday." Hugh rubbed the back of his neck where Steve had smacked him. "Anthony and I will take the eight o'clock train departing from the station."

Poppy dropped the tea tray with a loud rattle, her pink lips pursed. "That's too soon, our father just died, and you're worried about school."

"Poppy," Steve warned. Poppy simply glared back while threatening him with a butter knife. She would have made a good soldier.

Anthony looked at both of them. "Perhaps we should write to our schools—"

"No," Christopher interrupted. "School is important. You and Hugh are almost done with schooling. Father would not want you to fall behind, even with him—" he broke off. "He would want you to go back to school."

Anthony nodded, looking unsure as he looked at Poppy who looked like she wanted to rain terror on them all. Poppy narrowed her eyes toward him. "I can't believe you. Our father just died, and you want us to go back to how things were? What is wrong with you, Chris? Have you forgotten we don't have a father anymore?"

Hugh lit another cigar. "Enough of your hysterics, Pop.

Christopher is being levelheaded, something you need to work on."

"Say that one more time and I will burn your cigar through your eyeball, Hugh."

Hugh looked amused. "Which one?"

Lily burst into tears. "Stop fighting! Stop fighting! Daddy will be mad."

Christopher picked up tiny Lily and rocked her as if she were a baby even though she was too old for that. But she was a girl and the baby of the family, she needed comfort most of all. Christopher turned to look at Iris. "No one is fighting, Lily. Iris put Lily to bed she's overtired. Poppy, go with them you're too snappish right now."

Iris picked up Lily while Poppy threw one last evil look at them before the three girls disappeared up the stairs.

Steve handed his brother a glass of whisky. "I pity the fool who marries her. Our little Poppy is meaner than a wasp."

Hugh snorted. "Finn, if he ever grows a—"

"Watch it," Christopher barked as he finished off his drink. "Poppy is our sister, not to mention your twin. The pair of you will return to Laramie on Saturday and we'll see you back in Larkspur Valley in the summer."

"If there are no more tragedies," Hugh mumbled under his breath. Anthony shook his head.

Meanwhile, Steve laughed as he patted his older brother on the shoulder. "Don't worry, Christopher here won't let that happen. Right, Chris?"

Larkspur Valley, April 1870

. . .

Two months later Christopher Bennington had his hands full, and he felt like he and his beloved family were sinking to a point of no return, each member choosing to grieve in a different way. He was buried in paperwork and busy taking full reign of the ranching business, so he hardly slept. Steve was bedding a new whore at Madam Eugenia's whorehouse every night, sometimes two women at the same time. Hugh had gotten in trouble for punching two men across the face twice while drunk and the headmaster warned Christopher if he got into another fight between now and June he would not be graduating. Poppy was in an awful mood, she often shifted between fits of anger and making other people cry. Anthony's letters got more depressing each week. Iris spent all her time locked in her bedroom writing sad poetry. Little Lily had gotten so clingy with him she practically followed him to the washroom.

Christopher felt like he had aged twenty years in the span of two months. He often traveled back and forth from the main house, where his sisters continued to live, to his smaller bachelor house two miles down the road which his father had helped him build when he turned twenty-one for privacy.

"I'm awfully sorry about your daddy, Mr. Bennington," Chrissy Simon said when he answered the knock at the door. She practically threw a baked pie at his chest while her mother, Mrs. Simon, watched on with desperation as if hoping Christopher would propose right then and there. "Here, from me and Mama. Our famous blueberry pie, please share it with the rest of your siblings. Do let us know if you need anything, a bachelor with six siblings to take care of, one of them a mere child is too much to bear. I will gladly take care of Lily, I'm great with children."

"Thank you, though Poppy and Iris have Lily under control."

"Oh, of course!" Chrissy bowed slightly while giving him a toothy smile then she departed with her mother.

"Another pie, lucky you." Steve looked up from his cards once Christopher closed the door. They had been playing poker for three hours straight after they had made sure the girls were tucked in for bed. Steve and Christopher alternated spending the night at the main house with the girls even though they both agreed Poppy could do a better job of shooting at any intruder than either of them.

Christopher had a sour expression as he put the pie no one was going to eat on the kitchen counter. "Don't start."

Steve shrugged. "Chrissy is cute. You could do worse. The mother is a bit of a meddling witch, I hope you're prepared for that though."

Christopher ignored him as he began shuffling the playing cards. He didn't quite know how to say it, so he thought it best just to blurt it out. "I'm getting married."

Steve raised an eyebrow; he wasn't like Anthony who you could read like a book. "To Chrissy?"

"Don't be an idiot. I don't want to marry anyone in Larkspur Valley. Ever since Father died every marriageable girl between the ages of eighteen and twenty-five have been sniffing at my door with their mothers in tow." Christopher groaned. "I don't know how many more pies I can take."

"Not to mention you have a few spinsters who are clinging on your every word every time you tip your hat and say, 'good morning.' I can understand your frustration, thankfully I'm not the sole owner of the famous, well to do Bennington ranch."

"You're not a poor church mouse either." Christopher's voice was laced with sarcasm. "Father left all of us some money. Including the girls."

Steve smirked as he pulled out the king card and nearly shoved it at his chest. "But you're the prize fish they want.

Not the small fry. We won't inherit half of what you will. So, what's the plan? Go to a nearby town and court someone? That could take months, you know how fussy females can be. You barely have time to sleep, how are you going to court?"

Christopher reached into his jacket pocket and pulled out a newspaper titled, *The Matrimonial Market*, along with several letters. "I have placed an ad in this newspaper." There was an edge to his voice warning Steve he was not in the mood to be teased. "I will be sending for a mail-order-bride. It is the most practical choice. How it works is women across the country answer my ad and we exchange letters—"

"I know how it works." Steve looked at the dozen or so letters, some which smelled of perfume. "This is quite a gamble and very unChristopher like. What's the rush? Father died two months ago, technically we're supposed to be in mourning for another ten months. People will talk if they see you marry the first chit who responds to your desperate ad."

"Then let them talk. Being in mourning didn't stop half of the mothers from throwing their daughters at me."

Steve didn't say anything as he looked at the letters. "Why the rush? You've never cared about marriage before."

Christopher squeezed his fists until his knuckles were nearly white, a mix of embarrassment and frustration. "Because I'm thirty. It's time I grew up and start a family. Mother and Father had been married for eleven years by the time they were my age. I need someone to inherit the Bennington ranch since neither of you want to do it and Lily needs a mother figure. We can't expect Poppy to do it forever, she needs to marry and form a family of her own instead of fussing over us."

It was clear Steve didn't agree with his reasons for marriage, but he didn't say anything right away. He had always been quietly supportive like that. "It's your choice if you want to continue with this foolish idea. Have you picked one?"

"I've narrowed it down to these three." He pointed to three letters. "Minerva Judd, Judith Condron, and Lucille Robbins. I'm telling the girls tomorrow. The sooner they find out, the better."

Steve nodded wearily. "Poppy is going to kill you. She'll be furious you know. Maybe we should sign her up for *The Matrimonial Market* to finally get her married off."

"Poor Finn, he'll have a heart attack if we do." Christopher rested his back on the hard chair wondering for the tenth time since he placed the ad in the newspaper if he was making a grave mistake.

The next morning, after a Saturday breakfast of pancakes and eggs, Christopher dropped the news that in a few months, more than likely, his new bride was going to be arriving in Larkspur Valley. His three sisters stared back at him with round, blue eyes.

It had only been two months since the Bennington patriarch had passed away so technically his sisters should still be dressed in black, but after a month of mourning Christopher had ordered them to put their mourning clothes away. He hated seeing females in black. It was too depressing.

Lily had happily changed back into her purple dresses she loved so much, while Iris wore her usual dresses, but kept a black ribbon in her blonde hair in remembrance. The only one who didn't follow his orders was unsurprisingly Poppy who was still dressed head to toe in black, making her look older than twenty-five.

Right now, she was clutching a butter knife in her hand

and looking like she was about to stab Christopher with it. "You're an idiot."

Lily squeaked.

Iris snorted a laugh but was looking at her elder brother with a reproachful gaze.

"Poppy. Language." On more than one occasion Christopher determined his baby sister needed a good whipping and perhaps a mouth soaping. Not to mention a man to keep her in line. After his wife's death their father had spoiled her rotten which had made Poppy bossy, arrogant, and rude.

His right-hand man, Finn had spanked her once or twice over her dress skirts when she got a bit too out of hand. Finn had always confessed to him on the rare occasion he kept his baby sister in line, but Poppy always came back with a vengeance. She was a little hellion who was not going to be stopped by just one spanking. She needed constant discipline.

Iris spread butter on a piece of toast. "Chris, why do you have to marry a stranger? There are so many pretty girls in town. To have a strange woman here will be weird, wouldn't it?"

"Iris, that is not the point," Poppy hissed before she turned her blue eyes toward her brother. "Our father just died, and you decide now is the best time to get married?"

"I have my priorities straight. The summer is always the busiest time for me, the sooner I get married the better. Not to mention it is easier to travel in the spring and summer with our Wyoming winters. I don't expect you to understand, Poppy, but our father would have," Christopher replied coolly as he stared down at his sister. "I do not wish to marry anyone from town since the majority of the women, unfortunately, are simply after our good name or the wealth associated with it."

"And you think your little mail-order-bride will be as pious and humble as a nun? Be realistic, Christopher.

Women lie on those ads all the time. What if she has already been married? What if she had a child out of wedlock? What if she is the type of woman to open her legs to every man who will offer her money and a diamond ring?"

Lily's eyes widened.

"Poppy!" he snarled. "Enough. Nothing has been determined, but I will marry one of the three girls I mentioned sooner rather than later. I thought, as my sisters, you should have the courtesy to be aware of the situation. I have written to Anthony and Hugh as well."

"I suppose you want us to move out of the main house since Father is dead and you are to be a married man now. I'm sure your new bride won't want to share her new space with her husband's sisters."

"Now, Pop, don't be unreasonable. You girls can stay in the main house, we'll be comfortable in my bachelor quarters—"

"No, the *head* of the Bennington family deserves the main house for him and his new bride. We'll be out of your hair as soon as Finn and Steve help us move our stuff. I'm keeping Mother's jewelry box so do not even think about giving it to that little heifer you plan on marrying." She turned to Iris barking, "Get up, Iris, we need to pack so we're not in our dear brother's way."

Iris threw Christopher an apologetic smile even though she wasn't happy he was getting married either. She followed Poppy, leaving Lily behind at the breakfast table.

Christopher pinched her cheek. "You're happy for me aren't you, Lil?"

"Can I be a flower girl?" she asked worriedly. "I'm not too old, am I?"

"Of course not, pumpkin."

"What's her name?"

"Whose name?"

"Your bride."

Christopher paused. "I'm not sure. I have three choices, but I don't know which one I'll pick."

Lily bit her lower lip. "That's easy, you just pick the lady whose name sounds good with our last name." She was practically bouncing out of the chair. "What are their names? Tell me, then add Bennington as their last name."

"Minerva Bennington."

Lily shook her head. "It reminds me of Mrs. Minerva, the butcher's wife. She's always yelling. Minerva is an unpleasant name."

"Fine. How about Judith Bennington?"

Lily scrunched up her nose.

Christopher laughed as he tugged on his sister's blonde pigtails. At least Lily was happy for him. "You're running out of options, kid. Last choice: Lucille Bennington."

Lily rested her jaw on her little hand. "Can we call her Lucy? I like Lucy better than Lucille. Lucille is a grandmother's name. Lucy is the name of a bride." Christopher nearly choked on his laughter. "See Lucy Bennington sounds much better. Is Lucy going to be your wife?"

Chapter 2

BOSTON, *Massachusetts. April 1870.*

"Hurry, child, take this before that evil woman wonders what's taking you so long." Mrs. Ross, the baker's wife shoved a letter in twenty-three-year-old Lucille "Lucy" Robbins hand along with stuffing a loaf of bread inside a wooden basket.

Lucy retied the dirty apron twice over her very slim waist as she pulled the large dress nearly up to her neck in order not to expose her small breasts because she didn't wear either a chemise or a corset. She was quite lucky she even had a pair of drawers and that was only because Mrs. Ross had given them to her as a Christmas present. The green dress she wore, which was three sizes too big for her tiny frame, had to be stolen from the church's missionary barrel for the needy.

The small brunette woman did a curtsy as a gray bonnet shielded her pale face. She had lost so much weight in the past year she looked almost skeletal, you could see the outline of each bone on her oval shaped face and body. Her eyes were large, owlish on her discolored face and her lips too full. The only pretty thing, Lucy had decided about herself, was her long, curly brown hair even if it was kept up in a bun most of the time.

"Thank you, Mrs. Ross!" She curtsied three more times in gratitude before leaving the bakery.

"God bless you child." Mrs. Ross nearly sounded close to tears even though she wasn't an emotional woman. "May God have mercy on your soul."

When Lucy left the bakery, she walked down the familiar cobblestone steps leading to St. Bernadette's Orphanage for Girls. It was a large, gray building which seemed more suited for a funeral parlor than an orphanage.

Even though it had been Lucy's home since she was a baby the place still terrified her. She shivered whenever she saw it, though her shivering might have to do more with the cold and her hunger. Her stomach grumbled letting her know the hard bread she had had at breakfast wasn't enough to satisfy it. But it was all Mrs. Needles would allow her to eat.

Mrs. Needles was the headmistress of St. Bernadette's Orphanage for Girls and had taken over the throne after her husband had died at just twenty-eight. She had been the one who had found Lucy outside the orphanage crying in a basket with a note from her mother letting her know Lucy was born out of wedlock and therefore she couldn't keep her. Lucy's mother had written that she hoped her daughter would be adopted by a good couple.

However, Mrs. Needles considered herself a good Christian woman and determined babies born out of wedlock did not deserve a place in society and therefore should be punished for their parents' sins.

Lucy Robbins became an indentured servant for the

orphanage from the time she could walk which meant doing all the hard cleaning several times a day, wiping off the rain gutters, shoveling snow, doing errands for Mrs. Needles day or night, wearing dirty clothes, ripped shoes, and surviving on little food. Even the orphan girls looked down on her.

Everyone in Boston seemed to know about "Poor Lucy" but no one intervened because Mrs. Needles' brother was the Boston police chief, and he could make someone's life quite miserable if they made his sister unhappy. So, the people of this cold, harsh city learned to turn a blind eye when it came to "Poor Lucy." They ignored her growling stomach, the bruises on her face from the times Mrs. Needles took a break from using her beloved cane on her back and instead used it on her face, and the look of defeat in poor Lucy's eyes.

All except Mrs. Ross.

It had been Mrs. Ross who had come up with this foolish idea over two months ago toward the end of February when she suggested Lucy become a mail-order-bride for a bachelor out west and escape her hell. Lucy had been terrified at first, Mrs. Needles would surely drown her in the tub if she knew Lucy had even thought about escaping.

After gentle coaxing from Mrs. Ross and out of her own desperation she had finally agreed to consider it. Lucy didn't know how to read or write anything besides her name as she had never been allowed to attend school. Through small intervals Mrs. Ross had read inquiries to her about several gentlemen who were looking for a wife.

One finally caught her attention. A Mr. Christopher Bennington from Larkspur Valley, Wyoming. His post was sweet and simple. It mentioned he was the eldest of seven siblings who had taken over his family's horse and cattle ranch. Christopher was in search of a good Christian wife who desired children and who wouldn't mind hard work or living in a small town.

Lucy had known hard work all her life and after living in Boston since babyhood she would give anything for a quieter place to live. Mrs. Ross had wanted to look at other proposals, but Lucy had insisted on Christopher.

Mrs. Ross wrote him back with her neat penmanship and Lucy wished desperately she could read and write, but at twenty-three she was too old for school. The only reason her speech was so good was because Mrs. Needles would slap her across the mouth every time she used improper grammar. Lucy's letter to Christopher was short as well. She mentioned she had curly brown hair, that her favorite season was spring, she liked horses, but didn't know how to ride, and that she wanted three children.

Lucy had wanted to include the fact she was born out of wedlock, it was a big part of her identity after all and he had a right to know, but Mrs. Ross had declined, explaining it would cast her in an unfavorable light.

"You are a sweet girl." Mrs. Ross licked the envelope. "You do not need to be judged for your parents' sin. Let this man judge you for your heart, Lucy, not your birth."

Mrs. Needles had sent Lucy for the daily bread when Mrs. Ross had announced the first letter from Christopher Bennington had arrived from Wyoming. This time his letter had been a little longer. He told her about life in Larkspur Valley, assuring her he could teach her how to ride as he had taught his six siblings. He even included funny anecdotes about his siblings which made her want to get to know them. Lucy had never had a family. She never really had anyone except Mrs. Ross.

Christopher had ended the letter asking Lucy about her childhood, but she had already been running late and Mrs. Ross told her they would respond later before Lucy had stuffed the letter in the pocket of her dress.

"Move, stupid girl!"

Lucy had been too lost in her thoughts and hadn't noticed the orphanage's handy man and jack of all trades, Thatcher Watts bumping into her as he smoked a cigar while carrying an ax, no doubt Mrs. Needles had ordered him to chop something down. She hated trees and flowers.

She threw him a nervous smile which Thatcher ignored. He had been working for Mrs. Needles since Lucy was ten, he largely ignored her except on the rare occasions when he told the headmistress she should beat her up more.

Once Thatcher was gone, Lucy removed the letter from the envelope in her pocket and looked at it. Even though she couldn't read she still liked staring at the words. It reminded her that a rancher had taken the time to write to her and it made her heart swell. No one had ever shown interest before.

Before Lucy could scan the letter again, she felt herself being pushed down, her face slapping down against the cold concrete. She winced as she landed on her forehead causing her skin to tingle, yes that was going to bruise. Lucy managed to stuff the letter in between her breasts thanks to the large dress before the blows began.

She recognized the cane Mrs. Needles carried around at all times to punish unruly orphans, but in most cases, Lucy was her victim. The cane was heavy and harsh as it landed several times against her back. She felt the hard wood bruising her back with each punishing stroke. The strokes were cruel and delivered without an ounce of pity as the cane buried itself against her back.

"I sent you to the bakery an hour ago and here you are daydreaming!" Mrs. Needles roared, landing the cane three more times against the center of her back.

She hadn't seen the letter, but Lucy was in too much pain to pray for small miracles. The last stroke of the cane landed against her lower back. Mrs. Needles snatched the basket from her. "Clean yourself up you're a mess, you dirty girl," the headmistress ordered coldly. "Then serve breakfast, Lucy. Five minutes. No more."

"Yes, ma'am."

Lucy forced herself to stand up on shaking legs even though her skin was screaming in pain, no doubt bruises were already forming on her back. Mrs. Needles always liked hitting her on her back or the back of her legs because it meant Lucy would feel the pain with each movement she made, especially since she was made to work from sunrise to sundown.

Lucy's bedroom was in the attic of the orphanage. It was suffocating in the hot summers and freezing during the winter months, but it was the only place where she had privacy. Her hands trembled as she grabbed the pitcher of water, poured water into a bowl, then grabbed a washcloth to clean off the blood and dirt from her face.

Her bottom lip trembled when she saw her reflection in the cracked mirror. There was a bruise forming on her forehead which would be hard to hide, a scrape on her left cheek, and her lower lip was bloody. She looked ugly.

Suddenly, everything became too much for Lucy Robbins. She was tired of being kicked around and bullied by Mrs. Needles, tired of being treated like a pariah in the cold Boston streets because of the status of her birth, and tired of being plain, skinny, worthless Lucy.

She wanted love. Wanted a family. Most of all she wanted to feel safe and protected. If she stayed under Mrs. Needles' thumb, she would never achieve any of that. Her hand trembled as she pressed the cool cloth over her eyes. If she was going to survive, have a chance of a happy life then she needed to leave now.

"Lucy!"

"C-Coming."

Her hands smoothed down her dirty apron as she made

her way downstairs. The main problem was money. She didn't have any, except three pennies she had found one day while taking out the trash. And even if she could get money for her passage out of Boston where could she possibly go?

The letter, Lucy carefully removed the letter from in between her breasts. The words jumbled in front of her, but she could always find someone else to read her the letter. Lucy did have somewhere to go. She could go to Christopher Bennington in Larkspur Valley, Wyoming.

It was a foolish thought given that he didn't know her, and they had only exchanged letters once, but she was desperate and at this point she had no options. It was either go to Christopher and beg him to marry her, or at least help her in some way or live as Mrs. Needles' servant for the rest of her life.

Christopher had sisters, even if he chose not to marry her, he would at least help her. Wouldn't he? He sounded like a kind man.

Her mind was filled with thoughts and plans as she made her way into the kitchen to immediately cut fruit for breakfast. First Lucy needed to acquire money, then she needed to book her passage for an early train headed west, and finally she had to make her way to the train station without anyone noticing. Mrs. Needles would not hesitate to drag her back by her hair if she saw her in the train station.

For the first time since Mrs. Ross had read her Christopher's letter, she found herself smiling.

The following morning Lucy did not feel so cheerful as she had spent the evening tossing and turning trying to figure out a way to make money. It was a three-week journey from Boston, Massachusetts to Larkspur Valley, Wyoming. She would need money for several train and stagecoach passages, inns, and food. Money, she didn't have.

Lucy dragged her feet through the cobblestone steps on

the way to Mrs. Ross's. The headmistress had sent for another loaf of bread and this time she didn't dare spend an extra minute dictating another letter to send to Christopher. He would just have to be surprised when he saw her.

She stopped short when she saw a sign on a door. She couldn't read the sign, but someone had drawn a picture of a woman's hair being cut with numbers next to it. For some reason Lucy could not stop staring at the sign as she pushed open the door of the hairdresser's shop.

A plump, gray haired woman wearing a dress covered with bows was fussing over a set of combs. She wrinkled her nose as she looked at Lucy's dirty clothes. "Good morning, I'm Mrs. Fallon. May I help you?"

"I saw your sign outside. Could you tell me about it?" She was too embarrassed to admit she couldn't read. Very few people knew.

"There's not much to say. I buy hair."

"Buy hair?"

"Yes, for wigs. Women give me their beautiful hair, they get paid handsomely, and I make it into wigs. Are you interested?" Mrs. Fallon approached Lucy, suddenly looking interested in her brown glossy curls. "You have lovely hair, child. How long is it?"

"It reaches the back of my ankles, ma'am."

"Splendid. Quite lovely hair, I'm jealous. Would you be willing to sell?"

Lucy gasped as she clutched the chocolate brown tresses. Lucy Robbins did not consider herself a beautiful girl, she was rather plain, but she had always been proud of her beautiful curly hair. She had been about to reject Mrs. Fallon, but then she remembered how desperate she was for money.

"How much are you willing to pay?"

Mrs. Fallon gave her an amount. Lucy guessed it would

be enough for half of the journey. She touched her hair again, reminding herself not to be vain and that it would grow back. "Could you offer me a tiny bit more?" she coughed into her palm.

Her mind was racing if Mrs. Fallon offered her a tiny bit more then she could escape today. There was a train which headed out west daily on Tuesdays at nine o'clock given that Lucy had a tendency to overhear conversations since many people often forgot she was even in the room.

It was foolish to leave at the drop of a hat, especially since the money would hardly be enough to cover a journey to Larkspur Valley, but it was a start she could always figure out how to make money to cover the rest of the trip later on.

But she was sure of one thing Lucy could no longer stay in Boston, she had to leave before Mrs. Needles discovered her plan or she lost her nerve.

"It will be severely short if I offer you more money," Mrs. Fallon warned. "You'll look like a boy. It will be years before it would grow back to how it was."

A tear fell down her cheek as she thought about her chocolate brown curls. "I understand. Could you do it now, quickly?"

Mrs. Fallon nodded as she motioned to a chair in front of her. "Let me get my scissors."

Thirty minutes later Lucy Robbins nearly vomited when she saw her reflection in the mirror. Her beautiful curls were gone and in return she had short, brown pieces of thin hair sticking out in all directions above her ears. She was sure even men had more hair on their head than she currently had.

"Don't be so sad, sweet." Mrs. Fallon counted the bills before placing them in Lucy's hand. "Your hair will make beautiful wigs."

Lucy choked on a response as she took the money and

left the hairdresser. Once she was outside in the Boston streets her heart seemed to settle again. There was no time left for crying, she had to return to the orphanage, grab her meager belongings, and head to the station she only had two hours before the train departed.

In all her planning Lucy had forgotten about the bread she had been ordered to pick up. She had been awaiting another beating until one of the girls mentioned Mrs. Needles had gone to the local church for her weekly confession.

It only took Lucy ten minutes to place two dresses in an old saddle bag Mrs. Needles had discarded to her. She didn't have any other trinkets as she had never been paid for her work.

Perhaps God was finally on her side because she managed to sneak out once again. Lucy had stolen a sun bonnet from Mrs. Needles which was big enough to cover her shorn hair.

As she made her way to the train station it suddenly dawned on her she was leaving the city of her birth and the place where she had been so miserable. Lucy didn't have many people to say goodbye to, but she felt crushed she wouldn't be able to say goodbye to Mrs. Ross who had been her savior in many ways by her act of kindness. She made a mental note to have someone write to her from Larkspur Valley.

"I would like to purchase a ticket for Wyoming," Lucy blurted out to the man with the mustache behind the ticket counter.

The man stopped munching on peanuts. "You would have to take the nine o'clock train to Connecticut then purchase another ticket which will take you to Chicago, Illinois. In Chicago you would then board a train to Wyoming, then a stagecoach to this Larkspur Valley."

Lucy bit her lower lip so hard she almost bled. She touched Christopher's letter which was burning a hole in her pocket. "How long is the journey?"

"About three to four weeks give or take. It depends on the weather. Not to mention you're headed pretty far west."

"Please give me a ticket to Connecticut." She pulled out the bills Mrs. Fallon had given her and prayed the man had a good heart. Her arithmetic was slightly better than her reading and writing, but she had only dealt with pennies since Mrs. Needles had always been stingy. "Please help me."

"Of course, miss." The man took some of the bills then handed Lucy a thick, cream-colored ticket and returned the rest of the money. "Train leaves in an hour. You better sit down and wait for it."

Chapter 3

TWO WEEKS LATER. *Chicago, Illinois.*

She was running out of money.

Lucy came to the terrifying conclusion as she waited for the final train on her long journey. Her stomach was grumbling, and she was in desperate need of a bath, but she hadn't been able to afford an inn like the other travelers and had spent the days in between trains sleeping at the station to save money while waiting to continue the journey.

Her brown eyes watered as she looked at her drawstring purse. She only had two dollars left. Nearly the last of her money had been used to purchase the train ticket to Wyoming. But she still had to eat and pay for the stagecoach to Larkspur Valley.

Lucy rested her back against the hard bench suddenly feeling very foolish. She was about to break down in tears due to her poor thinking when she suddenly heard a familiar voice.

"Where's your outhouse?"

That voice, she turned around and saw a familiar figure a few feet away. Thatcher Watts. The handyman and jack of all trades back at the orphanage. What was he doing in Chicago?

He had always said he would head out west to make his fortune someday, but Lucy assumed it had been drunken talk. What were the odds they would end up in the Chicago train station at the same time? As far as Lucy knew he had no plans to travel anytime soon.

Lucy clutched her little purse to her chest as if waiting for a beating or for Mrs. Needles to pop out of nowhere and drag her back to Boston. She watched the interaction between Thatcher and one of the workers from the station carefully.

"Out back. The furthest part from the station, sir."

Thatcher snorted as he grabbed his things and headed to the outhouse. Lucy waited a few minutes before following after him. She clenched her stomach at what she was about to do. She was about to steal from Thatcher.

Lucy gave a silent prayer asking God to forgive her, trying to make Him understand she really had no choice. She was dangerously low on money, and she still had a week and a half to go. Her plan to do menial tasks for money had flown out the window when she realized most of the jobs were only available to men or at least women taller and healthier than Lucy.

Lucy crouched against the wall as she peeked at Thatcher through the corner of her eye. The men's outhouse was empty. Thatcher grumbled about the cold as he made his way inside the outhouse. It was ridiculously small, meaning he had to leave his small bag outside which is what Lucy wanted.

As soon as the door closed Lucy scampered toward the bag like a cat. Her heart was racing as her trembling fingers opened the bag. Thankfully, Lucy had always had quiet feet and quick fingers. She opened the bag, thanking the Lord, Thatcher was still messy.

Lucy found several crumpled bills; she stuffed as many bills as she could in the pocket of her dress not bothering to look at them. Ten minutes later she boarded her final train headed to Wyoming.

Once she was in her third-class passenger seat, hopefully safely away from Thatcher she reached into her dress pocket to count the bills. A gasp escaped her lips. It was a hundred dollars.

"Are you all right, miss?" the train conductor asked worriedly as he looked at her pale face.

Lucy nodded as she stuffed the money in her drawstring purse. If Thatcher ever found out she had been the one to steal the money he would kill her. The sheer possibility he might even be on the same train as her was enough to give her goosebumps.

But Thatcher had always mentioned when he went out west, he would head to California. She hoped it was still true. Lucy stared out the window seeing Chicago nearly fly past her, still in wonder by modern transportation methods.

In about a week and a half she would be in Larkspur Valley where she would see Christopher Bennington for the first time. Maybe it was youthful hopefulness or complete stupidity, but she hoped from the bottom of her heart that this kind stranger would marry her.

By mid-May Larkspur Valley was experiencing their first hot days, indicating that summer was around the corner. Christopher had just received a letter from Anthony and

Hugh but even that didn't seem to put a smile on his hard face.

Anthony had finished his third year of Divinity school with flying colors and would be spending the summer with his family instead of going on another mission trip like he had for the past two years. Christopher was happy to learn he sounded more upbeat since his last letter.

Hugh had mentioned in the letter the date of his June graduation from medical school. After graduation he was planning on returning to Larkspur Valley to intern under the elderly Dr. Peterson who had offered his practice to the young Bennington once he retired.

Christopher had been surprised Hugh had chosen to return to town, but Hugh had mentioned he hated the city. The eldest Bennington knew it was his younger brother's way of saying he missed his siblings, not to mention there were very few people who tolerated him, ergo the nickname "Evil Twin."

However, the thought of his younger brothers coming home did not bring a smile to Christopher's face. He had been rather depressed and filled with self-pity for the past few weeks when he hadn't received a letter from Lucille Robbins.

Poppy had been ecstatic at the notion of course while Iris and Lily had been more sympathetic.

"I can't believe you're still moaning over a chit you didn't even meet." Steve was less than sympathetic as he pushed a glass of whisky toward him on Saturday afternoon once the brothers had gathered at the local saloon. It was barely four and Christopher had dismissed the workers early, which was a rare occurrence. "You exchanged what, one letter? That's not enough for a broken heart."

"I just thought she would have had more decency than just not responding to my letter," Christopher continued to grumble over the music. He snapped his finger to order another glass from the busty saloon girl.

"You expected a lot from a city girl. Especially a mail-order-bride. You should have just picked a local girl." Steve looked at him as if he was the stupidest man on earth. "Cheer up, big brother. Order as many drinks as you need tonight to help you forget about this Lucille girl, I'll tell them to put them on my tab."

Lucy Robbins arrived in Larkspur Valley on the six o'clock stagecoach feeling exhausted, sweaty, and dusty. She desperately wanted a bath to make herself presentable. Lucy had used some of Thatcher's money to freshen up in Laramie, but the journey had been long.

But the day was slowly coming to an end. Tomorrow was Sunday and more than likely the Bennington family would be at church, not to mention it would be highly improper to storm in on a Sunday uninvited. She was already pushing it, as far as she was concerned.

She touched the short, brown curls which were sticking up underneath her sunbonnet. It had hardly grown during the near month-long journey and as a result she hardly removed it out of shame.

Lucy gripped her small satchel in her hands as she headed to Simon's General Store where the stagecoach had dropped her off. If anyone knew where to find Christopher Bennington it would be the owner of the general store.

Her brown eyes looked around Larkspur Valley hastily. This was her first visit to a small town, and she couldn't help but glance at the picturesque view. There were rows and rows of buildings, carefully tended to streets despite the dust, surrounded by vibrant green meadows that no doubt bloomed with flowers in the spring and summer.

"Can I help you, miss?"

Lucy had been too busy looking at her surroundings and she'd hardly noticed she had entered the busy store. A middle-aged man wearing a gray vest with a thick mustache was behind the counter waiting for her patiently.

"Hello, I'm Lucille, um, Lucy Robbins. I just arrived from Boston and I'm looking for Mr. Christopher Bennington. Would you mind pointing me in the right direction?" she stuttered, hoping the general store owner didn't think she was a strumpet for looking for a man when she was clearly unmarried.

The man ran a hand over his bald head. "It's about a twenty-minute journey from here. He lives in the outskirts of town. It's too far to walk, you need a wagon or a horse to get there."

"Oh, I thought he lived nearer to town." Though it did make sense he lived further away given he owned a ranch.

The man shook his head. "Nope, Bennington owns the third largest cattle and horse ranch in the state of Wyoming. Him and his family practically own half of Larkspur Valley, richest family in town."

"R-richest?" she stuttered.

She'd guessed Christopher had some money when he mentioned he owned a ranch and was sending for a mail-order-bride while taking care of all the expenses, though she had never expected having to ask the richest man in town to marry her.

Lucy flushed, feeling sick to her stomach as she took in her dirty dress, her overly thin body which had become even thinner throughout the long journey, oh and her poor hair. It would be a miracle if Christopher Bennington didn't run away screaming.

The tears started pouring down her face. Stupid. How could she have been so stupid to think a prominent man like him would marry a poor, uneducated bastard? She might be twenty-three, but here she was acting like a delusional little girl who had listened to too many fairy tales.

There was no way she would return to Boston, but maybe she could get a job here. She still had the majority of Thatcher's money and if she was careful, she could make it spread until she got a job.

But gone were the dreams of being a bride. Of a love story worthy of a romance novel. Lucy was a fool. Foolish girls had to take the consequences of their foolish actions.

The man looked uncomfortable at her crying. "Miss, please don't cry. It really is not far. The sheriff, Steve Bennington is his brother I'm sure he will take you to his brother's ranch." The door of the general store was pushed open. "Oh, actually there is someone who may be able to take you, don't cry, miss. Mr. Weston, a word if you please."

Chapter 4

LUCY STOPPED SOBBING when the owner called over a tall, blond man with an athletic built holding the hand of a little girl. The little girl couldn't be older than ten or eleven, her blonde hair was in thick braids, and she was dressed in an expensive looking purple and green dress.

The blond man tipped his hat forward. "Afternoon, ma'am. How can I help you, Mr. Simon?"

Mr. Simon looked extremely relieved to see this Mr. Weston. "Mr. Weston, I'm so relieved to see you. Miss Robbins here is looking for your boss. Would you mind accompanying her? She's new to town and didn't know the ranch is further away."

"My brother isn't at the ranch, he went to see Steve. Finn and I came to buy candy for Poppy and Iris," the little girl said, and turned to Lucy and gave an elegant curtsy. "I'm Lily Bennington, pleasure to meet you. I'm the youngest Bennington, there are seven of us."

Lucy couldn't help but choke out a smile. This child was adorable not to mention overly polite. "It's nice to meet you,

Mr. Weston, Lily. I'm Lucille Robbins, but please call me Lucy."

Finn gave her a polite smile. "Miss Robbins, we will be happy to take you to—"

"I know who you are. You're Lucy!" Lily started crying out while she jumped up and down. She pointed an accusing finger toward the brunette. "You're Chris's bride, he said he was going to bring you to Larkspur Valley so you could marry him. What took you so long?"

Lucy blushed, apparently this child knew more about her than her own groom. Finn looked embarrassed, meaning he knew something about the letter she and Christopher had exchanged. Mr. Simon was obviously curious, but manners forbade him from inquiring further.

"It was a long journey."

Sensing her discomfort, Finn draped his heavy coat over her thin body and took her satchel. She felt both relieved and ashamed of his gentlemanly nature. She hated feeling like a charity case even though she was.

"I'll drop you off at the house, Miss Robbins. I'm sure Mr. Bennington's lovely sisters will be able to keep you company while I search for him. Let's go, Lily. I'll let you drive the horses back home, only don't tell your brothers."

"Finn," Lily stomped her foot. "I want my candy, you promised. I'm sure Lucy wants some candy too."

Finn sighed, obviously no match for the youngest Bennington. "All right, pick some candy, Lily. Mr. Simon, please put it on the tab."

"Of course."

Five minutes later, Finn, Lucy, and Lily were back in Finn's wagon. Thankfully, Lily was a chatterbox and she quite happily talked over any current awkwardness. By the time they arrived at the second Bennington home Lucy knew all of Lily's brothers were working in vastly different professions, that Christopher liked chocolate the best out of all candy, and that according to Lily she was the favorite because she was the baby.

Lily had just been about to launch into a discussion about her seventeen different dolls when Finn interrupted with a wince, "Lily, honey, how about we let Miss Robbins have a break? I'm sure she has some questions as well."

Finn Weston, Christopher's right-hand man had been extremely polite to her, a true gentleman, but it was obvious he was bewildered about this entire scenario. This made Lucy feel even more stupid and if she had been clever enough to come up with a plan B she would be running in the opposite direction by now.

"We used to live in the main house before Daddy died," Lily announced as she held Lucy's clammy palm. "Poppy said we had to move to Chris's old house because Chris needed the bigger house for his wife and babies."

"Lil," Finn groaned, obviously embarrassed by the youngest Bennington's bluntness.

"That's what Poppy said!"

"Well, Poppy has a big mouth," Finn mumbled, a slight blush coating his cheeks.

Lily barged in before either Lucy or Finn could knock. The house smelled of cinnamon and fried dough which made Lucy's mouth water. Her stomach growled in protest, letting her know she was hungry.

Finn cleared his throat in greeting as a fifteen-year-old girl stepped away from the stove. *This must be Iris*, Lucy thought recalling Mrs. Ross had mentioned Iris was the middle Bennington daughter. She was petite and willowy with a long golden braid down her back. She was cleaning up her hands with a cloth napkin. "Finn, Lil, you two are back so soon."

Before either of them could say anything, they heard the

footsteps coming downstairs. The voice was sharp reminding Lucy of a stern headmistress. "Iris, is that Finn? He better not have spoiled Lily's dinner, I specifically told him he—"

A tall, blonde woman in her mid-twenties reached the bottom of the staircase. Poppy Bennington. The blonde was taller than Lucy with golden blonde hair pulled back into a tight bun. She was dressed in a severe looking black dress with a large onyx mourning brooch at the collar of her dress, resting above her heavy bosom.

Her expression did not seem to soften when she noticed her guest. She planted her hands firmly on her hips, her voice cold. "And who is this?"

Finn cleared his throat. "Iris, Poppy, Miss Robbins has just arrived in town looking for Christopher. Mr. Simon asked if I could bring her here while I search for your brother, Lily mentioned he was with Steve."

"I'm Lucy Robbins." Lucy grinned nervously at them. "Pleased to meet you, I am thankful for your hospitality."

Iris gave her a small smile, but she was looking nervously at Poppy who was still staring at Lucy as if she were a cockroach.

"And what is your business with my brother?" Poppy asked coldly.

"Poppy, be nice," Finn warned. The oldest Bennington female ignored him as she stared at Lucy as if she were her latest prey.

Lucy fiddled with the ribbons of her sunbonnet, not noticing she was causing it to slip backward exposing the short, brown curls. Iris gaped, but Lily didn't seem to notice.

"She's Chris's bride." Lily started to excitedly dance around. "I told you she would come, Poppy."

"Don't be ridiculous, Lily." Poppy turned coldly to Lucy, ignoring her baby sister's crestfallen face. Poppy obviously recognized her name even if they had never met. "As if my brother would ever marry this raggedy, ugly urchin who looks like she crawled out of a sewer." She looked at Lucy's worn-out brown dress with the green stripes. "From the looks of it, this little beggar is just after our brother's money like they all are."

Lily stared at the two women as if she didn't know who to believe. Iris blushed but didn't stop to defend her. Lucy's eyes watered with tears as her cheeks burned with humiliation. Poppy Bennington was right in some way, she was a poor, uneducated young woman who was looking for her brother as her savior. But did she have to be so harsh?

Behind her Finn was gritting his teeth as he glared at Poppy. "I warned you, Pop to hold back your tongue." He gripped the blonde's upper arm as he dragged her up the stairs while Poppy screamed and flailed to get away from his strong grip.

Ten seconds later, Lucy, Iris, and Lily heard girlish hollering along with a hard palm meeting a skirt covered bottom several times. Iris blushed, looking embarrassed that Lucy had to witness it while Lily simply shook her head as if the little girl was used to hearing the arguing between Finn and Poppy which was now elevating with each smack. Lucy would be surprised if people all the way in town didn't hear her shrieking.

"Poppy is naughty sometimes, so Finn spanks her even though she's bigger than me." Lily brightened. "I never get spanked, Lucy. I'm a good girl."

Lucy chuckled nervously, not sure what to say as Poppy's hollering and cursing turned into meek sobs. Finn came downstairs a few minutes later looking hassled while a bright handprint painted his left cheek.

Iris gasped as she inspected his cheek. "Oh, Finn, did Poppy slap you?"

"She nearly tore my eye out, but I warned your sister not

to be a rude brat like she always is. It's not my fault she didn't listen. I'm going to find Christopher. Lily, Iris, please keep Miss Robbins company."

Then with a tip of his hat toward the girls he headed outside again while Lucy stayed behind wondering what she had just walked into.

***

"Why did our mother and father have too many siblings, one brother is more than enough." Christopher knew he was drunk, by the way his words slurred, yet he kept drinking even though he was going to have a major headache tomorrow. It didn't help that Steve, who could drink like an elephant, kept serving him glasses of liquor while he didn't look the least bit tipsy. Maybe the fact that Lucy hadn't written to him hurt him more than he would ever admit.

"Don't let the others hear you say those words," Steve warned. "You know how jealous they can be especially the twins. Every day I'm convinced they could run a small dictatorship with their tempers alone."

Christopher paused. "Well, I guess Anthony, Iris, and Lily are rather sweet. I couldn't imagine life without them."

"All right then we'll just get rid of the twins."

"Are you two seriously drunk before eight?"

Christopher and Steve turned around to look at Finn who was looking at them with a disapproving look. The head of the Bennington family pointed to his cheek. "What happened there?"

"Your sister," Finn responded flatly. "She has a mean slap."

Steve laughed. "What did you do, propose for the hundredth time? I already told you, Weston, you will not get her to marry you even if you were the last man on earth."

Finn scowled at him. "If you must know I had to spank her. Over her skirts of course to preserve her modesty and only using my hand."

Steve snorted as he poured himself another drink. "Then you didn't do a very good job. Everyone knows a good punishment is always conducted on the bare."

Finn ignored him as he turned to Christopher who was trying and failing to stand up on his jittery feet. He was going to kill Steve tomorrow if he couldn't even get up without vomiting. "The reason I spanked her was because she was being incredibly rude to your guest, a Miss Lucy Robbins who just arrived in town."

Christopher burped. "It can't be Lucy. My mail-order-bride never responded to my letter."

His right-hand man tapped his foot impatiently. "And I'm telling you Miss Robbins is in your second home looking for you. I'm not sure if it's the same Lucy, but the possibilities are slim that it's a different one."

Lucy? Lucy was here? Christopher stood up on staggering feet as if Finn had announced Santa Claus was waiting for him at his front door. "I have to go see her." Steve had to hold on to him to make sure he didn't fall.

Finn gave him a dirty look. "You are as drunk as a skunk. You cannot meet a lady in this state."

"Who made you Miss Manners?" Christopher snarled.

"Gentlemen, please." Steve stood in between them. "I say we should let Christopher say his greetings to Lucy so he can make sure it's not a figment of his imagination, excuse himself saying he's not feeling well, and meet her properly the next morning while he's sober. Miss Robbins can stay with the girls tonight. Lily has an extra bunk bed."

Chapter 5

"DID you enjoy your time in Boston?" Iris asked politely as she placed her teacup back on the plate. Lily had soon grown bored of their "grown up" conversation and was playing with her dolls while Poppy was still sobbing (or plotting) upstairs leaving Iris and Lucy alone.

Iris was being extremely polite to Lucy, much nicer than Poppy, but Lucy could tell she didn't trust her. Lucy didn't blame her, she had barged into their lives after all as a complete stranger with the plan to wed their older brother.

"Not really," she finished awkwardly, not wanting to tell her about the orphanage or Mrs. Needles when Iris already seemed terrified of her. "It's too cold, I heard Wyoming is a bit warmer."

"It is. Won't your parents miss you for having traveled so far?"

"My parents are dead. I worked—used to work in an orphanage."

Iris looked embarrassed. "I'm sorry. I didn't mean to bring up painful memories. I know firsthand how heartbreaking it is to be an orphan."

That's right Iris had lost both of her parents before she was a grown woman. To Lucy, that somehow felt worse since Iris at least knew what it felt like to be loved while she knew what it was like to grow up alone.

The front door opened, and Finn came staggering in along with two men. They were both handsome with coal black hair and big blue eyes. The slightly shorter one was holding the taller man upright as if preventing him from falling.

Lucy's smile faltered though she wasn't sure if it was because of nervousness or disappointment. Both men were obviously drunk even if the shorter one looked slightly more sober. The taller one who was struggling to walk broke apart from his younger brother's grip.

"You're Lucille, Lucy," he managed to say as he ran a hand through his thick hair.

Iris balked behind her. Apparently, she had never seen her older brother this intoxicated either.

"Yes." Lucy cleared her throat as she managed a small curtsy. "I'm Lucille Robbins, nice to meet you. And you are?"

"Christopher. Chris. What are you doing here? You never responded after my last letter," Christopher blurted out.

Lucy fidgeted, unsure of what to say. She didn't want to confess her thievery and that she'd been running away from Mrs. Needles' beatings in front of all these people. "I thought I would come to meet you. Getting to know each other in person is more intimate than exchanging letters, don't you think?"

"Sweetheart, Boston isn't exactly around the corner."

There was an awkward silence before Finn pulled on his boss's arm. "Miss Robbins, please excuse Mr. Bennington he is indisposed at the moment. He wasn't expecting you, I'm sure he will properly greet you tomorrow." Christopher argued for a bit before Finn practically pushed him out the door. "Steve, would you please help Miss Robbins settle in?"

Steve smiled sheepishly. "Sure thing. Good evening, Miss Robbins. I'm Steve Bennington, sheriff of this fine town."

Once Finn and Christopher were out of the picture Lucy stayed behind looking at her black shoes. She wiggled her toes feeling the ripped men's socks she wore. She bit her lower lip so much it nearly bled. "I shouldn't burden you any longer. I need to find an inn in town. I thank you for your hospitality."

Before she could move, Steve gripped her arm. "You're not staying at an inn. You came all this way to meet my brother who, I promise, is more high strung than what you currently witnessed. We have plenty of room, you will stay here with the girls."

"It really is not necessary."

"I insist, Miss Robbins. Please don't make me threaten you with jail if you do not." Steve was smiling, but something about his tone indicated to her that he was not joking despite his smile.

Not wanting to appear rude, and not finding a good enough reason to not accept his hospitality, she wearily agreed. Iris then told her she had prepared a bath upstairs if she wanted to bathe, Lucy readily agreed wanting to escape the Bennington siblings.

As she reached upstairs, Lucy heard Steve and Iris talking. Steve's voice was soft, he didn't seem like the type to lose his cool. "I heard from Finn that you and Poppy were incredibly rude to Lucy."

"Poppy more than me," Iris argued. "You can hardly blame me, Steve. She storms in out of nowhere wanting to see our brother. Didn't you see her? Her clothes are dirty, and she has hair like a boy."

"Iris, you forget not everyone is as lucky as you. Where is our devil sister?"

"Upstairs."

"Sulking no doubt. She always sulks when Finn spanks her. Brat. Lucy will be staying the night, we'll decide what to do with her in the morning when Chris is sober. I'll be downstairs if you need anything. In the meantime, please be kind to her. The poor girl is terrified to death."

"She is nice. The journey from Boston was rough. She's an orphan too."

"Lovely. We have that in common. Go to bed, Iris, none of us want any dinner."

"Yes, brother." A pause. "I still don't want her to marry Chris though."

"It's too soon to talk about marriage. We'll discuss it in the morning."

After her bath Lily insisted Lucy should share the extra bunk bed in her room which had once belonged to the twins. Lucy had agreed. Out of the three Bennington sisters, Lily was the sweetest.

"Lily, how is Christopher?" Lily looked confused until she elaborated. "Is he funny? Kind? Smart?"

Lily started braiding her long, golden hair. "Steve is the funny one. Hugh is the smart one. Anthony is the sweet one. Christopher is," Lily paused. "Christopher is the strict one."

Lucy hugged the pillow to her chest. "Strict?"

"Yes, he's very stern." Lily's small face was serious. "He has all these rules we need to follow, and he gets mad when we disobey." A smile appeared on her face. "I'm his favorite though. He swore me to secrecy."

Lily then fell deeply asleep while Lucy squirmed uncomfortably in the bed. She couldn't sleep. She kept thinking about Christopher greeting her drunkenly, how Lily had described him as strict. Would he be as strict with her too?

Were his siblings covering for him? What if he got drunk every day?

The Benningtons might be a prominent family, but that did not mean they did not have their own skeletons in their closet. The last thing she wanted was to be the wife of a drunk. Lucy hadn't escaped one hell to go into the arms of another.

Her teeth bit her lower lip, once again hating herself for how stupid and delusional she had been. Of course, this whole mail-order-bride plan had been an absolute sham. Lucy turned to her side, hugging her knees close to her chest.

Tomorrow she would leave.

Lucy was not sure where she was going to go. All she knew was she was getting the hell out of Larkspur Valley.

———————————————

Chapter 6

———————————————

"HERE, DRINK."

Steve handed him a cup of strong coffee which caused Christopher to wince. He still drank it even though the back of his head was pulsing painfully. The next time Steve offered him alcohol he was going to punch him.

"Where's Lucy?"

Steve raised an eyebrow. "So, you do remember your little mail-order-bride. I thought Finn's head was going to explode when he dragged you out of the house yesterday."

Christopher nodded as he finished his coffee. It would be hard to forget little Lucy Robbins. She was a slip of a girl who looked younger than twenty-three with dirty clothes, an overly thin body, and the curly brown hair of a twelve-year-old boy.

He grew embarrassed when he remembered how he had drunkenly insisted he had to meet her even though Finn told him he was making a mistake. The look of disgust on her pale face was burning a hole in his mind. That was not the impression he had been hoping to make, but then again what was she doing here? She was not supposed to be in Larkspur Valley after she had ignored his last letter.

Christopher ignored his pulsing headache as he took another sip of coffee hoping it would cure his hangover. Steve offered him another cup and he shook his head.

"Your little mail-order-bride stayed with the girls. They were still sleeping when I came to wake you. Hopefully, our dear little Poppy hasn't sliced her throat yet."

Christopher ignored his twisted sense of humor as he finished dressing, put on his hat, and saddled his favorite horse, Artemis. The Benningtons' second home, his old bachelor home was only fifteen minutes away by foot.

When he entered the house, he smelled bacon. Lily was nowhere to be seen, so he guessed she was upstairs dressing. Iris was setting the table with a confused expression on her face while Poppy cooked the bacon. The blonde was whistling which was never a good sign. It meant she was being mischievous.

"Good morning, girls." He cleared his throat.

"Good morning, Christopher," Poppy responded cheerfully as she put the bacon on a plate. "Would you like to join us for breakfast?"

"Not right now, Pop. I would like to speak to Lucy, where is she?"

"Gone." Poppy sounded almost gleeful. "She ran like a thief in the night. When Lily woke up, she was no longer in the bunk bed."

Christopher turned to look at Iris just in case his younger sister was lying. "Iris?"

Iris shifted from foot to foot. "It's true, Chris. We looked everywhere, but when we woke up this morning Lucy was gone. Maybe she went back to town."

"Good riddance." Poppy grinned.

Christopher glared at her. "Not another word, Poppy or I

will ask Finn to finish what he started yesterday." She glared at him but didn't bring up the subject again.

Sensing his sisters couldn't be more help, he left the house in search of Lucy Robbins. He was ninety percent sure the little fool was running around lost somewhere. The Bennington property was large and there were miles and miles of empty fields surrounding them.

You needed a horse or wagon to get into Larkspur Valley, otherwise it was an hour journey on foot. *She couldn't have gotten far,* he assured himself as he got on Artemis again and started heading west. *I'll find her.*

Lucy was lost.

There was no other way to put it. She felt like a sheep going around in circles. She had been walking for thirty minutes and still she was nowhere near town. Her feet were getting tired, and she was very close to bursting into tears. But she had to keep going unless she wanted to die from starvation or dehydration.

The sun was beating down on her face even though it was only mid-May and quite possibly not even breakfast time. She had slipped out around dawn while the Bennington sisters were still asleep. Her plan was to go into town and get the first stagecoach or train out of Larkspur Valley.

She had made her peace that she was going to go to a new town, find a job, and remain a spinster for the rest of her life. Of course, thanks to her Lucy luck she was currently stuck in the middle of empty country with no idea where she was going.

Lucy had been close to bursting into tears when she heard her name being called.

"Lucy! Lucy!"

She flinched as she went down on her knees, wrapping her arms around her head like a scared rabbit. It was Thatcher, she was sure of it. He had somehow found out she had stolen his money and was out for revenge.

"What on earth are you doing?" the male voice asked incredulously.

She opened one brown eye to stare at Christopher Bennington looking incredibly handsome on top of a horse. He was staring at her as if she had just lost her mind. Maybe she had, after all she had come to this small Wyoming town after exchanging only one letter with the man.

Lucy stammered, "I thought you were someone else."

The confusion turned to a scowl. "You shouldn't have left my sisters' so early in the morning. The open country is large, you could have easily gotten lost and walked for miles without a soul in sight. As it turns out you've been walking around in circles, you silly goose. It didn't take me long to find you."

"I-I," she faltered unsure of what to say. She was suddenly feeling less brave in front of the scolding, angry looking man who had greeted her while drunk last night. Perhaps she'd prefer the drunk version, he was less scary at least.

He raised a dark eyebrow. "Yes?"

"I changed my mind. I don't want to get married anymore," she mumbled, looking at her feet.

"You came all this way just to change your mind?" His voice softened. "Look, Lucy, Miss Robbins you are due an apology. I behaved very poorly last night; you deserved a proper greeting. I assure you it is not my usual state. It was a one-time fluke. It will never happen again. Please forgive me."

She nodded. "Thank you for apologizing, Mr. Bennington."

"Christopher or Chris."

"Pardon?"

"After our meeting last night, I rather doubt we have to follow formalities and we can use our Christian names." His lips twitched slightly. He had a very handsome smile. "Don't you agree?"

She nodded shyly as she played with the sleeves of her dress. "Yes, um Christopher, I know it was rather ill mannered of me to arrive without notice or a formal introduction. Please accept my apologies as well."

Christopher looked uncomfortable at her meekness as he got down from the horse. "Lucy, we should go back to the main house. We will have more privacy there, don't you agree? We have much to discuss."

Lucy hesitated, she didn't have a proper chaperone, but after traveling all the way from Boston by herself it seemed rather silly to be worried about having a chaperone. Besides Lucy's past was hardly a fairytale. The less witnesses the better. She nodded quietly.

Christopher offered his hand to help her on top of the horse and Lucy took it. Before he helped her sit on top of the horse, however, he did something unexpected. He bent her over slightly, using one of his bulky arms to steady her while his other hand rose in the air.

Before Lucy could even question it, six sharp smacks landed on her small bottom, all of them landing straight down the center of the fullest part of her cheeks. Her dress and drawers were thin making Lucy feel every stinging swat. The slaps had been delivered fast, but they still left behind a throbbing pain in their wake.

Lucy whimpered as her lower lip trembled. She felt like a naughty little girl as Christopher rubbed the sting away with the hand that had just been used to deliver the punishment. Lucy had never been spanked before as Mrs. Needles had preferred beating her across her face or on her back. She certainly never thought she would be spanked as an adult woman especially by a man who she thought would be her fiancé.

"That was for leaving without telling anyone where you were going," Christopher said simply, as he placed his hands around her waist and plopped her on the saddle causing Lucy to squeak. "Don't do something which could put you in dangerous situations, Lucy. The world is not always a kind place."

Lucy was about to respond quite sassily back that if anyone knew about how unfair the world could be it was her. But that was before Christopher settled himself behind her, wrapping his arms around her lithe body as he held the reins.

She felt his hard muscles against her back, his strong thighs caressing her waist, and inhaled his manly scent. Even though she had only known this man for less than twenty-four hours Lucy felt her heart pounding inside her chest as her body grew warm.

This had been the first man she had ever gotten close to. Lucy had a feeling Christopher Bennington would be the last man in her life.

Chapter 7

THE MAIN BENNINGTON home was simple, but pretty, made out of thick wooden material with pretty glass windows. It was two stories high with a wraparound porch and several potted plants at the entrance. Much more welcoming than the orphanage she had grown up in.

As soon as Christopher helped her down, she excused herself to the washroom feigning that she needed to freshen up, while in reality she wanted to look at her spanked bottom. Thankfully, the washroom had a large full-length mirror edged with gold.

Lucy hiked up her thin dress skirts and pulled down her shabby drawers thinking it was one of the pros of being poorly dressed. A small gasp escaped her lips when she saw the state of her creamy buttocks. On each cheek there was a large, pale pink handprint decorating it as if marking its territory.

Her fingers traced the handprints wincing when she touched the darker pink areas. Was Christopher's hand truly that big? How had he managed to subdue her in under five minutes with a simple spanking?

Being spanked felt different than when she had been beaten by Mrs. Needles. The head of the orphanage had beaten her out of cruelty and spite, taking pleasure in it. When Christopher had done it, he had acted as if it was a chore that needed to be done. He had been quick and efficient to correct her naughtiness and, to be honest, she didn't know how to feel.

She knew children were often spanked by their parents, but she had never heard of a husband or potential husband spanking their wife.

Lucy was once again caressing her rear end when she heard a knock on the door.

"Lucy, is everything all right in there?" Christopher sounded suspicious as if he thought she had climbed out the window like a monkey.

"Yes, I'll be right there." She put down her skirts, then pinched her cheeks to add some color to her otherwise colorless face and headed into the sitting room. Which was decorated in different shades of blue and green, sprinkled with knick knacks, and homemade art projects. No doubt the work of his sisters because Christopher did not seem like the decorating type.

Her heart fluttered when she looked at Christopher. He was just so handsome, how could she have been so lucky? *Don't count your chickens before they hatch, Lu,* she scolded herself. *This is how you ended up in this situation in the first place.*

"Sit down." He pointed to a blue velvet chair. His voice was not cruel, but definitely authoritative. The kind of voice that ran a whole ranch and didn't have the patience for wayward young girls.

Lucy did as she was told, a squeak escaping her lips when her sensitive nates touched the hard seat. Even though her spanking had been short and sweet, Christopher definitely knew how to leave an impression.

His lips twitched as he sat across from her, but he had the decency not to comment. He crossed his long legs. "Now, Miss Robbins we finally have some privacy. How about you tell me the story about how we went from exchanging letters to you landing on my doorstep like a pretty little package?"

Lucy blushed. Had he really called her pretty? No one had called Lucy pretty before. She gripped the worn-out dress skirts, avoiding looking at him. "I just really wanted to meet you, and I thought what was the point of waiting when I could—"

"Lucy," Christopher interrupted once again calling her by her Christian name and not the proper Miss Robbins. "Know this, if there is one thing I don't tolerate from anyone it's lying. So, please be honest with me or it could end up very badly for you."

Her brown eyes widened, his brother was the sheriff after all. "Are you going to throw me in jail if I lie to you?"

Christopher burst out laughing. "Of course not. Lying is not a crime, but mark my words, you will end up with a sore tush with the spanking you'll earn if I find out you fibbed."

Lucy's cheeks turned red, there was that word again. Spanking.

The brunette squirmed. Before she knew it everything was spilling out of her mouth, "My mother abandoned me at an orphanage when I was a baby because I was born out of wedlock. Mrs. Needles runs the orphanage, and she made me an indentured servant of sorts." Her palms started becoming sweaty. "It was a miserable life. I worked from dawn to sunset for no wages. I've never received schooling. I don't know how to read and write. Compared to your siblings I am very uneducated and plain."

Christopher touched her neck gently, caressing an old purplish bruise. "Did she do this to you?"

"Yes, my skin is very fair. I bruise easily."

"How did you start writing the letters, or should I say letter, if you don't know how to read or write?"

"Mrs. Ross who owns a bakery helped me. She knew being a mail-order-bride would be my only chance to escape. No one would court me in Boston and since I am uneducated, I have limited options." Her eyes watered as she remembered the last beating she had received. "I couldn't take life at the orphanage anymore, so I decided to leave. I sold my hair to be able to afford the trip here." She decided to leave out the stealing part of her journey, she couldn't imagine what Christopher was thinking with the information she had already given. "I apologize for dropping in unannounced, but I couldn't wait. I completely understand if you do not wish to marry me. We hardly know each other after all and it's not fair for me to pressure you into a marriage with a girl you hardly know."

"Lucy, look at me."

She looked up and saw Christopher was leaning forward looking at her gently with his blue eyes as he squeezed her rough hands. "You've been very brave, I doubt many people would have been able to go through what you went through. Thank you for your honesty." He didn't speak for a moment, but when he did his voice was low. "In my advertisement I mentioned I was looking for a woman to wed who was a good Christian woman, who wanted children, and was fine with being a rancher's wife. Does that sound like you?"

Lucy hesitated. "Yes, but—"

He raised a dark eyebrow. "But what?"

"I was born out of wedlock," she whispered. "I'm uneducated. When I wrote to you, I had no idea the Bennington family was so prosperous. Otherwise, I would have never dreamed of writing to you."

Christopher grinned. "You make us sound like royalty when we are just average folk. As for your birth I do not care about your origins, it is not your fault. We can teach you to read and write, my sister Iris has it in her head that she wants to be a teacher and my evenings are free. What I am trying to say is I don't care about your past, Lucy, only our future. I am open to marry you if you still wish. If you do not, then I will help you settle in town and we'll go our separate ways."

"You will marry a complete stranger?" she whispered, still in shock about how nonchalant he was about her miserable life. Anyone else would have run away screaming not wanting to get involved with a damaged orphaned girl.

He gave her a sheepish grin. "One of the reasons why I turned to *The Matrimonial Market* was because I did not want to go through the courting process. I simply want a wife who will help me run the ranch and will give me children. I ask for nothing more."

Lucy bit her lower lip. "What about love?"

"If we are destined to love then it will come naturally," he chided her cautiously. "But I am a practical man, Lucy. It might never happen for us. Marriage for me is about partnership rather than love. Rest assured I will protect and cherish you. Give you a roof over your head, all the food you can eat, I will take care of our children. You will have a good life, Lucy."

Lucy nodded, trying not to show her disappointment. She was too old to believe in fairytales, but she would be lying if she denied that a part of her had been expecting extravagant declarations of love. Christopher was describing it as if it were a business deal. But he was also right in a way, marriage was primarily about partnership, not love, and he had sworn to give her and her children an honest life. Perhaps love was not in the cards for her, if she said "no" then what would her life be like?

"Lucy? What do you say?" he asked her. "If you are unsure—"

"I'm not," she choked out. "Yes, Christopher, I will marry you."

For the first time, since they sat down to discuss the arrangement, he smiled. "Excellent. My brother Hugh will be graduating from medical school in two weeks and Anthony is coming home for the summer. After they return to Larkspur Valley, we will marry about the second week of June. Will three weeks be enough for you to obtain a dress in which you want to be wed?"

Lucy could only nod, still trying to register the fact she was due to become Mrs. Bennington, a rancher's wife in three weeks. Everything was going so fast she could hardly swallow. "That should be fine. Should I rent a room in an inn? It won't be proper for me to stay here even if we are engaged."

"Of course not. You'll stay with my sisters in the second house." He saw her face fall and he assured her, "Don't worry about Pop, her bark is worse than her bite. If she gives you any trouble let me or Finn know and we will deal with her. Iris and Lily will help you get settled, and let any of us know if there is anything you need for the wedding. You already met Steve and Finn."

She nodded as she touched her bare wedding ring finger.

Christopher must have noticed this because he blurted out, "You will get my mother's wedding and engagement ring. I will have to take it to the jeweler's to get it resized." He frowned as he studied her small, rough-looking hands. "Your hand is so small."

Lucy nodded as she tugged on her bonnet wishing her beautiful hair was long so she could appear dainty and feminine instead of sickly and plain. "Thank you. I promise I will treasure it and we can pass it off to our son for when he finds a girl to marry." *Which hopefully won't be like this.*

Christopher patted her cheek and she was surprised

when she leaned forward as if begging for his caress like a spoiled kitten. "Thank you for your understanding, Lucy. I've never married anyone before, and I don't exactly have anyone to give me advice." He stopped as if he were suddenly remembering a painful memory. "There is something we must discuss. I gave you a light spanking earlier this morning for leaving without telling anyone where you were going. If you agree to be my wife, then you must be aware that spanking is part of the deal." Her brown eyes widened. "That being said, Lucy, you can still back out."

Lucy coughed as she started to fidget. "I didn't say I wanted to back out, but I want you to explain more." She took a deep breath. "I've been beaten my entire life by Mrs. Needles, I will not be a beaten wife, Chris."

Christopher surprised her by pulling her into a hug as he rubbed her back. "You poor thing, you've had a rough life, haven't you?" He surprised her by kissing the top of her head. "Lucy, I will never beat or scar you in any way like Mrs. Needles did. A spanking is just that, a spanking. I will slap your buttocks or the back of your thighs like I did when I found you wandering around like a lost sheep. But never to the point of bruising, you're just going to be walking around with a sore tush for a day or so."

"But why?" she squeaked. "Why can't you just scold me?"

"Because as your husband it is my job to discipline you when you need it." He tipped her chin up so she looked at him. "And sometimes the offense requires a sore tush."

She wrinkled her nose. "Offense?"

"Lying. Putting your life or anyone's life in danger willingly. Being unkind, that sort of thing. If you are a good girl then you have nothing to worry about." He pulled back. "My father spanked my mother, not often, but only when she needed it. It made their marriage stronger. It is not for everyone, I agree, but if we are to be married, Lucy, then being spanked is part of the deal. I require your obedience, in return I will make sure you are cherished, respected, and never want for anything."

You forgot loved, she wanted to cry out, but she didn't, even though her lower lip trembled. Maybe it was her destiny to never be loved by anyone, even a husband. As for the spanking, she had taken worse from Mrs. Needles so as long as she behaved, she had nothing to worry about. Lucy had always been good at following orders after all.

"I understand about the spanking. Yes, I will still marry you."

"Excellent." Christopher helped her up. "Let's go back to the second house. Poppy will have breakfast ready. Then I will take you and the girls into town to get anything you need. Clothes, shoes, a new bonnet. Whatever you want, I have accounts in all the stores. You can charge whatever you want within limits, and I will pay off the account next time I see them."

Lucy suddenly felt ashamed of her poor fitting clothes, torn shoes, and ugly sunbonnet which was doing a poor job of hiding her short brown curls. "Oh, you don't have to do all that. I have some money——"

"Save your money, Lucy. What's mine is yours now." His tone was firm and left no room for arguments. "I will take care of your expenses now, I will even give you some pin money weekly. There's no need to be embarrassed, you already spent a small fortune traveling here from Boston. Besides you will need a wedding dress."

Lucy nodded as he wrapped his hands around her waist and placed her once again on top of the horse. He followed close behind and she wrapped her hands around his strong, muscled arms with fear she might fall.

She closed her eyes, feeling his strong abs hitting her

small back. Lucy Robbins was to be married. For better or for worse. Lucy just hoped this time the gamble she had taken wouldn't backfire.

The next few days passed by in a blur as she spent more time with the Benningtons and Finn. Though Poppy kept ignoring her and even more so when her brother gave her their mother's old engagement ring, a simple gold band with a pretty emerald in the center.

Iris and Lily were nicer to her though and they helped her plan the wedding from choosing the flowers for the church to coming up with a menu for the wedding breakfast. Only a handful of people knew the oldest Bennington was getting married as Christopher wanted to avoid the busybodies which served Lucy fine as she hated loud crowds. Her wedding dress had been picked out from one of the ready-made dresses, the dressmaker had to choose from.

The weeks flew by and before Lucy knew it Christopher, Steve, and Poppy were heading to Laramie to pick up Anthony and for Hugh's graduation from medical school. Christopher had wanted Lucy to come along, but after weeks of traveling across the country she begged to stay home.

Iris and Lily were staying with her because Iris had school while Lily was too young. Finn was keeping an eye on them even though the Benningtons were only gone for a week.

Once Christopher came back, he and Lucy would be married. Her stomach flipped at the thought of her being married to a man whom she had only known for a couple of weeks. Steve, Iris, and Lily had warmed up to her and included her in their conversations, sometimes they even managed to tease her. Poppy still scowled at her, but wasn't as cruel as in their initial meeting, no doubt because she wanted to avoid another punishment.

The only one she was still unsure of was her husband as

luck would have it. Besides his initial drunken greeting, Christopher had been a polite gentleman by visiting her every evening, taking her shopping for new clothes, and giving her compliments though Lucy knew she resembled a walking skeleton even though she now had plenty to eat.

But there was something missing.

Lucy couldn't put her finger on what it was, but it was bothering her, or maybe she was acting like a vain, idiotic child. After growing up the way she had, she should be grateful she had a man who was treating her kindly, but often she would long for that affection between couples in love. The sweet pet names, the giggling, surprise kisses on her cheeks. The most Christopher did was hold her hand and even that was only for a few seconds.

More times than she cared to admit, she thought back to how his hand had felt across her bottom when he had punished her. Then she would scold herself for being so perverted for thinking about a man's hand across her rear end.

He didn't ask her about her childhood or Boston because he knew it was a painful topic for her, but then again he didn't ask her much of anything besides what she thought about Larkspur Valley or how the wedding planning was going.

Lucy sighed sadly as she got ready for bed the day before Christopher, Poppy, and Steve left for Laramie. She feared that, while Christopher would keep his promise and be a protective husband, their marriage would be a dull one.

Stupid, Lucy. She bit her tongue as punishment as she crawled into the bed of the guest bedroom she was staying in. *First you complain that you want a stable, quiet married life then you complain you want more excitement. No wonder Mrs. Needles and Thatcher were often annoyed with you.*

She said her prayers and curled into bed thinking of things she still had to do for the wedding.

Lucy was back at the orphanage. She was freezing and crying in her attic bedroom, the warm clothes Christopher had bought for her all but a distant memory. She had never left. She would never leave. Mrs. Needles owned her, she reminded her of this often. Her own mother hadn't wanted her. Why would a successful man like Christopher Bennington even look in her direction? Let alone marry her?

She saw two people approaching her attic bedroom. One of them was Thatcher, his little eyes furious as he looked at Lucy. Then there was Mrs. Needles who was carrying the familiar cane she adored so much.

Lucy felt her body stiffen as she looked at both of them. One was the man whom she had stolen from and the other was the woman who had made her miserable since she was a baby.

"Is this her?" Mrs. Needles barked. "The thief?"

Thatcher nodded as he licked his cracked lips. "That's her all right."

"Thieves get punished, Lucille." And then she raised the cane.

"Lucy! Lucy, for heaven's sake wake up. Ow!"

Lucy opened her eyes only to see Poppy holding her by the shoulder, staring at her with wide, confused eyes. There was a thin, pink scratch across her cheek from where Lucy had scratched her.

Poppy was so pretty, she looked like one of the ladies from the magazine covers. She wondered why she wasn't married, then again Poppy could probably crush any man she deemed unworthy without any help from her brothers.

The blonde Bennington was staring at her with a mix of confusion and concern, this was probably the first time she wasn't scowling at her. She knew Poppy was angry at her brother for marrying a girl born out of wedlock and uneducated, but Christopher had simply told her to shut up and to butt out of his business.

"I'm sorry," she stammered. "I didn't mean to."

Poppy ignored her apology. "You were screaming the house down. I'm surprised Iris and Steve didn't hear it. Were you having a nightmare?"

Lucy rubbed her neck looking for the familiar bruises given by Mrs. Needles' cane, but they had long since disappeared. "Something like that. It was about my time at the orphanage."

The blonde sucked in her breath. "Was growing up in the orphanage really that bad?"

It was the first time Poppy had spoken to her without any malice. It was a bit odd. "Yes, Mrs. Needles was a cruel woman. She used to beat and starve me just because she could. She did it for twenty-three years."

"What a cunt."

Lucy burst out laughing. It felt odd that such a horrible word could come out of such a pretty mouth. Despite her beauty, she could swear like a sailor and Lucy wished she could be more like Poppy, not the swearing part, but being able to have the confidence to say anything without caring what others thought.

"Yes, she was." Lucy suddenly felt shy. "Poppy, I know you don't like me, that you don't think I'm a good match for your brother, but I promise I will try my best to make him happy and be a good wife to him. I am grateful for his care."

Poppy sobered up, but didn't acknowledge her statement. "Christopher has a lot on his plate. He's been in charge of us since he was nineteen. He does not need any more problems, so please tell me you will not cause him any."

She thought about how she stole the money from Thatcher and hoped the man was in California like he had planned all along.

"I will not be another burden to him," she whispered.

Relief crossed Poppy's face as she finally relaxed. Despite

her hard exterior, Poppy cared deeply about her family. It was the reason why Anthony, Iris, and Lily practically thought of her as "mother" even though she had only been fourteen years old when she had been forced into the role.

"You should get some sleep," Poppy said, her voice was almost kind. "It's past two in the morning and you'll need to help Lily get ready so Finn can take both girls to school."

School. Lucy wondered what that was like. She had never had the opportunity to attend and couldn't help but feel a little jealous. "Of course." Before Poppy could leave, she questioned her about a matter that had bothered her since her first day. "Poppy, do you have any feelings for Finn Weston? He's always around."

Poppy's face darkened, not with anger, but with embarrassment. "Finn is Finn. He's Chris's best friend which is why he's always here. Nothing more. Now go to sleep before you make me cross."

Chapter 8

LUCY FINALLY MET Anthony and Hugh the day before she was to be married. Her soon to be husband had mentioned Hugh was here to stay after graduating from medical school and was thinking about opening his own practice the following year while Anthony was only staying for the summer as he still had one more year of Divinity school.

Even though they were brothers, Anthony and Hugh couldn't be more different. Anthony had delicate looking features like an Italian sculpture. He was also very shy and extremely polite, a vast difference compared to his older brothers.

Hugh was Poppy's twin and once she met him she finally understood why the pair of them were called the "Evil Twins." Hugh, while more polite than Poppy, had a cold, detached personality. Even when he smiled, his smile never seemed to reach his eyes, and he had a nasty smoking habit. His skin was extremely fair like his sister's which often burned in the hot Wyoming sun. But while Poppy had golden locks like a porcelain doll, Hugh's hair was as jet black as his brothers' though his eyes were an icier blue.

They were both handsome, but Anthony was definitely friendlier to Lucy than Hugh who seemed indifferent.

"The ceremony will begin at nine," Christopher informed Lucy after their family dinner as Lucy stood by the doorway feeling both shy and excited at seeing her fiancé again after not seeing him for a few days. "Pastor James will perform the ceremony. I'll pick you up at eight-thirty."

"No," she blurted out while he looked confused. "It's bad luck to see the bride before the wedding. I asked Finn to drive us to the church, well me and the girls since Iris and Poppy are my bridesmaids and Lucy the flower girl."

Christopher looked like he was about to argue about what he surely thought was a silly tradition before he saw Lucy's pleading eyes. "As you wish. I will meet you at the church then. Did Finn take your stuff over to the main house?"

She nodded, though it hadn't been much. Only a small trunk containing the new clothes he had purchased for her. She was still wearing a bonnet everywhere even though her curly hair now reached her ears.

There was an awkward silence as Christopher cleared his throat and Lucy fidgeted, both of them no doubt dreading this awkwardness would follow them for the rest of their days. Lucy broke the silence by gently patting his upper arm. "I'll see you tomorrow then."

Christopher kissed her forehead, instead of her lips, while Lucy tried to hide her disappointment. "Until tomorrow, Lu."

"What's taking so long?" Christopher asked moodily as he paced around the church in his Sunday best suit feeling that the material was hot and scratchy compared to his usual work clothes. "She's supposed to be here already. Finn promised he would bring her on time. She's late. Lucy is never late, she is always obnoxiously prompt."

The church was nearly empty as Lucy and Christopher decided not to invite anyone besides the family and Finn. As his best man, Steve was standing next to him looking amused at his misfortune. Anthony was talking excitedly to Pastor James while Hugh sat on a pew looking bored.

"Will you relax? The bride is always late, it's tradition. Do I need to get you smelling salts?" Steve joked while his older brother glared at him. "Are you sure you want to do this? Lucy is a sweet girl, but you've only known her for a few weeks and she sort of ambushed you. No one would blame you if you called it off."

Christopher pointed to his three-piece suit. "It's a little late for that. Besides, I made a promise to Lucy. I don't break promises."

Steve nodded, not looking entirely convinced as the double doors opened. "Here comes your girl."

Finn threw him an apologetic look as he found his seat. Lily dressed in a buttercup yellow dress and a flower crown started throwing daisies, oblivious to the crowd behind her. Poppy and Iris dressed in matching yellow dresses fussed over Lucy one last time while Hugh waited to take his place, he was going to walk her down the aisle as the third oldest.

Christopher took a deep breath as he heard the rusty organ start to play rusty music. His three sisters were coming down the aisle, but he hardly paid any attention to them. All his attention was focused on Lucy who was hugging Hugh's arm as if her life depended on it.

His bride was dressed in a cornflower blue dress with a large sash and bow to hide her thinness and lack of womanly hips. Christopher made a mental note to feed her all of her favorite foods for the next few months to have her gain weight for the cold winter months which would greet them once the summer ended. The blue dress had a wide draw-string collar made of the palest blue material which matched the ruffles on the tight sleeves and the bottom part of the dress.

Lucy was holding a simple bouquet of white roses with lavender flowers tied with a matching blue ribbon. Her dark, curly hair was still painfully short so she had borrowed a pale blue hat with a white ribbon which belonged to Iris.

She was looking at him shyly which made his manhood stir in his pants, something which definitely should not happen at church. Even though he'd been speaking to Lucy every night since she had arrived, this was the first time Christopher felt he was really looking at her. Her pert little nose, her rosy cheeks, and her full lips which she kept biting out of nervousness which only seemed to make them redder.

For a second, the entire church disappeared. He could only look at his soon-to-be wife. After today they would be bound. Forever.

Pastor James had to clear his throat twice while Lucy gently stepped on his foot for him to turn around so the cere-mony could begin. Pastor James cracked the Bible open. "Dearly beloved, we are gathered here today to join this man and this woman in holy matrimony."

The ceremony lasted an hour and finally the pastor spoke the words he had been waiting for. "You may kiss your bride."

Christopher turned to look at Lucy who had turned an adorable shade of red. She was looking at her new blue shoes. Poor thing was so shy, Christopher doubted she had ever held hands with a man. His cock jumped in his trousers at the thought.

Calm down, he scolded himself, *you'll scare her away.*

He leaned forward since she was smaller than him,

pressing his lips against her own soft pink lips. Lucy eagerly followed his movements instead of shying away like he had been expecting.

Lilac, vanilla soap, and cinnamon greeted him as he kissed her. He wouldn't mind sleeping to those scents every night and those lips. Those wonderful, pillowy lips he never wanted to stop kissing.

Christopher's tongue was just beginning to poke through her petal pink lips to caress the inside of her plump shaped mouth when he heard someone clearing their throat from behind. He turned slightly looking at Steve winking at him while Pastor James gave him a dirty look.

Lucy let out a small squeak as she clutched her small bridal bouquet.

The Bennington family and Finn clapped politely as he led his bride through the church's aisle while Lily threw the remaining flower petals at them. Lucy gave him a small smile which he returned with pride. It was done.

The rest of the morning and mid-afternoon went by smoothly. Poppy seemed to have gotten over whatever animosity she'd had with Lucy and was actually helpful during the wedding breakfast.

Christopher felt himself relax as the hours went on, content he had made the right decision as he watched his bride talk with Anthony and Iris. He had made a good choice in picking Lucy as his bride. She was sweet, helpful, and obedient. The perfect person to be a rancher's wife.

At half past two, Christopher told his family he was taking his young bride home. Steve started wolf whistling which earned him a rare slap against the back of his head by Hugh.

"You seem surprised by the house," Christopher teased her as he watched Lucy's wide-eyed expression. "But you've seen it before."

She giggled. Maybe it was the fact they were finally married, but she had grown less shy and more receptive to his advances in the past few days. Christopher couldn't wait until the day she was finally comfortable in his presence.

They entered the house and Christopher gave her a little tour since he hadn't done so before. He showed her the sitting room, his study, the basement, the attic, the kitchen, storage shed, and then he led her up to the second floor where seven guest bedrooms and one main bedroom awaited. His father had built them each a bedroom even though it was common for siblings of the same gender to share one.

"What will you want my role to be?" Lucy asked warily as she looked over the row of bedrooms, probably wondering if she and Christopher would have this many children. Which was amusing as well as endearing.

"You'll take care of the housework, cooking, laundry, housewife duties." He ran a hand through his dark hair. "Maybe in the future I will teach you how to milk a cow and feed the chickens, but those can wait for now. Come, honey, let me show you our bedroom."

He took her to the main bedroom which was located on the far east side of the house. The room was large, but cozy and made of expensive looking smooth wood. There was a large bed in the center covered with a cream and lavender colored bedspread. There were two green and white quilts at the edge of the bed and many fluffy, goose feather pillows. Christopher had even added a large vanity table with an oval shape mirror with a row of drawers for beauty supplies. On top of one of the large chest of drawers there was a vase where she could put her bridal bouquet.

"It's lovely." She turned toward him, stumbling with her words while the redness started blooming in her cheeks. "I thought, well, are we going to share a bed?"

"We are," he said firmly, moving toward her to brush away a stray brown curl. "I know the start of our marriage was less than traditional, but the rest of our marriage, Mrs. Bennington will be very traditional. Which to me means sharing a bed every night unless one of us is sick or you're giving birth to our children."

Lucy looked at him with big brown eyes reminding him of an adorable sparrow. "I like it when you call me, Mrs. Bennington. It feels nice to finally be married."

He chuckled as he started pressing his lips gently across her cheeks before heading down the crook of her neck. "Mrs. Bennington, Mrs. Bennington, my lovely Mrs. Bennington."

It took all his willpower not to press his wife against the bed and ravish her, but first they had to have an awkward conversation Lucy should have had with her mother or her mother-in-law. However, since neither lady was alive it was up to him.

Christopher took a deep breath, he needed to be careful with how he presented the words. Lucy was innocent. The last thing he wanted to do was scare her even though his manhood was practically threatening to crawl out of his pants.

"Lucy, come sit down on my lap." Christopher sat down on the bed and pointed to his knee. Lucy hesitated for a bit, probably thinking he was going to punish her again, but eventually she sat on his lap. He wrapped his arms tightly around her pressing her tight little body against his. "Lu, do you know what happens between a man and woman in the marriage bed?"

She hesitated. "They kiss?"

God, her innocence was adorable.

"They do." He pressed a hand against her bony knee, she

didn't push him away instead she leaned her body closer to him. "But they also do other things. Naked."

She took a deep breath then started stammering. Apparently, she had thought this little marriage of convenience would be them ignoring each other, but alas if either of them wanted children they needed to know each other very intimately.

"What kind of things?" Lucy finally managed to ask.

Christopher rubbed his chin, unsure of how to bring it up without scaring her. "My male organ gets bigger when we are ready to perform the marriage act." He pointed to his crotch which was already becoming unbearably tight. "I place it inside you when I part your flower open."

He wanted to punch himself for being so stupid. Flower? Male organ? If Hugh or Steve were here they would laugh in his face by how foolish he sounded.

But Lucy was peeking at him with interest, curiosity, and dare he hope a little bit of desire shining in her brown eyes. "Will it hurt?"

"A little, the first few times," he admitted as he squeezed her hand. "But then it will get better, sweetie. I promise I will try to make you feel good."

"Will it hurt less than a spanking?" He didn't know if she was teasing him or if her question was genuine, but he couldn't help but burst out laughing.

"Probably."

She nodded as she looked at her lap before turning her face to him while tugging on a brown curl. "Christopher, can we try doing it now?"

He nodded, fumbling around like an inexperienced young man. By the way he was acting if was as if he had never been with a female. But if he was being honest with himself it had been more than a year since he had lain with a woman. Steve preferred visiting brothels, Hugh seemed to have a preference for lonely married women or widows, and Christopher couldn't sleep with a proper woman without marrying them, so he chose to remain abstinent except on the rare occasions when his brother dragged him to a brothel.

Christopher pulled her in for a kiss and he felt her relaxing in his arms. It seemed Lucy enjoyed being kissed by him if how she was reacting now was any indication. He could feel her nipples turn into hard little pebbles under her dress as she unconsciously started rubbing her body against him.

She stiffened a bit when he started unbuttoning her wedding dress, but Christopher relaxed her by caressing the inside of her mouth with his tongue. Her blue dress went to the floor leaving her in her corset, chemise, and dozens of fluffy petticoats.

Her rough looking hands immediately went toward her small bosom, but he pulled them down gently. "Don't hide yourself," he warned her gently. "I want to see every inch of you."

"I want to see you, too," she shyly admitted, leaving her arms firmly against her sides as instructed.

His fingers started unbuttoning his white dress shirt exposing the hard muscles on his chest which were covered in dark, velvety black hair. His chest and forearms were large, almost bear-like and he suddenly felt like a giant next to tiny Lucy.

Lucy sucked in her breath, but she didn't shy away from him. Instead, she pressed her hand against his chest. Her fingers interlocking against the fine chest hair as she studied it with a curious expression. It was more than likely the first time she had seen a nearly naked man which made him feel possessive.

Christopher allowed her to play with his chest for a bit

before he started unlacing all the frills and ribbons which made her look like a plump wedding cake. Once she was nude, Lucy stood back trying her best not to shield herself even though every part of her body was growing red with embarrassment.

Lucy was extremely thin, to the point he could see her collarbone and her frail ribs poking out, even though she had been living with the Benningtons for the past few weeks. He made a mental note to ask Hugh how he could plump her up before the winter came even though Lucy said she had always been small boned. Christopher wanted to strangle the headmistress of the orphanage and equally starve her so she knew what it felt like. The fact Lucy felt no anger or resentment toward Mrs. Needles, at least from what he saw, made him feel as if he had married an angel.

Lucy's breasts were small with strawberry pink nipples which were becoming hard little rocks the more he stared at his wife, it was like they were trying to show off. She pressed her pale thighs together guiding his attention to the patch of soft brown curls hiding her womanhood underneath its snugness.

Christopher trailed one finger against the patch of soft curls against her mound causing her to shiver. "Beautiful," he murmured. "You are simply beautiful, my Lucy."

Lucy stared at him in wonder. No doubt the poor thing had never been called beautiful before. "Do you really think so? Even when my hair looks like this? Do you truly think I'm beautiful?"

He tugged on a brown curl before he kissed her forehead. "In my eyes you are the most beautiful girl in the world, Lucy. I will remind you of this every day."

"You're quite handsome, too. I'm lucky I married you," she blurted out before shyly looking away.

"I'm the lucky one for having you be so brave and searching me out."

Christopher started peppering her neck with sweet kisses, his warm hands going from her neck to her breasts to gently caress them. She didn't pull away, instead she arched her back forward as if pressing her bosom to his chest.

Her skin was soft, her breasts tender as his lips kissed every inch of her bosom roughly until pinkness started to bloom under the pale skin from his ministrations. A whimper escaped her mouth as she ran a hand through his dark hair.

He pressed his hand underneath her small bottom before pulling her forward. She opened her legs to straddle him, her pink pussy lying on top of the hard muscles of his stomach. The eldest Bennington sibling almost came when he felt the soft, female organ pressing against his body.

Lucy was wet. Hot. Practically drenching all her sweet juices against his lower body as if coating him with her scent. Whimpers transformed to moans as she dug her nails against his neck, while she rubbed her naked breasts against his hairy chest, desperate for more friction.

"Hold on to me, Lu," he grunted as he managed to unbuckle his trousers and let them and his underthings fall to the floor while he still held a naked Lucy in his arms. His erection nearly jumped out of his trousers. It was hard, angry, and purple.

It rubbed itself against the bottom of Lucy's buttocks causing her to let out a low gasp in surprise mixed with a bit of apprehension.

Lucy blinked her brown eyes as she looked at Christopher's throbbing erection as it covered her skin with its pre-cum. "It's big. I didn't realize it was going to be quite like this," she finished awkwardly, her skin becoming red as she inwardly cursed herself for her lack of intelligence.

Christopher seemed to find her adorable though because

he let out a wolfish laugh as he slapped each of her thighs gently while raising her up in his arms, and pushing against her sweet bottom so she could rub herself against his entire torso to cover it with her sweet scent.

"Don't worry, baby." He nibbled on the bottom part of her earlobe. "It's less scary than it looks, I promise I will be gentle."

"Can I touch it?" Lucy suddenly blurted out. Her eyes were still fixated on the organ which would pierce her delicate flesh in a matter of minutes.

Christopher looked at her with a mix of pleasure and desire as he grabbed her hand and led her down to his shaft. His wife let out a surprised giggle as she wrapped her hand gently against the veiny member, feeling it slippery and hot against her hand.

She rubbed her hand up and down, as if she were holding on to a broomstick, which caused the blood to flow to his prick as it jumped underneath her innocent exploration. "Does it hurt when it's like that? It looks swollen."

"No. Well, a little," he admitted. "But it's a good feeling. When it's like this, swollen, it means it wants to be inside here." He pointed to her lower lips which were nearly coated with her sweet cream.

"Oh." She wiggled her hips. "Then maybe we should remedy that."

Christopher laughed in delight at her innocence, she was talking as if they were discussing chores they had to do around the house. He kissed her again before he gently put her on the bed on all fours with her bottom up in the air.

She looked perplexed as he ran a finger across her sensitive back which was filled with the old marks of wounds made by Mrs. Needles. He would talk to Hugh and check if there was some cream or ointment which would help the marks disappear. Christopher wanted to press charges against Mrs. Needles, but he didn't want to make Lucy go through an entire stressful ordeal. He would wait a few months, once they were both settled to discuss it with her.

"This position is better for your first time," he announced with a smile as he gently spread her legs open to look at her weepy cunny. She was as swollen as him. "It will give you more room to move around without me pressing my body against you. Lu, I promise you I will be as gentle as possible. If you want me to stop at any time, tell me, honey."

She nodded. There was a slight nervous smile on her face, but she didn't pull away.

Christopher gripped her hips, reminding his hot headed, lustful self how delicate his new wife was. The head of his cock pressed against the soft petals of her sex parting her open. Christopher started piercing her open with his organ, with one hand still gripping her hips, he used his other hand to rub her clit.

She started moving her butt, her bottom rubbing against his chest as the pleasure started growing in between her legs.

He grunted when he felt a delicate piece of flesh preventing his cock from going in further. Her hymen.

Christopher took a deep breath as he pushed himself forward in one quick stroke destroying her hymen and filling her with his cock. Lucy let out a yelp as two tears slipped from her eyes and her bottom lip started trembling.

His hand started rubbing the bundle of nerves between her legs with more haste, wanting the moment of pain to disappear. A kiss went to the back of her head. "We're done, sweetie. The hard part is over. It's only pleasure from now on. Okay?"

She nodded slowly as Christopher positioned himself further into her, until her bottom was practically pressed against the front of his thighs. He started fucking her slowly, letting her get used to his length and girth.

His hand started caressing her breasts, alternating between pinching her nipples and squeezing them gently under his heavy hand. He pounded inside her, less gently than at the beginning as he filled her with every inch of his cock. His thighs hit her roughly as the sound of skin slapping against skin entered the room.

Lucy started panting as she opened her mouth while her body shivered. "Oh, Chris, I feel like my stomach is going to explode."

"Relax your body, Lu. Scream if you want."

Christopher smirked as his bride did as she was told and allowed her orgasm to enter her body at full force. Her body trembled as her breasts swung below her.

His breathing was heavy as his heart nearly jumped out of his chest as his orgasm coated every nerve of his body. Pressing his hands against the mattress he looked at Lucy, searching for any signs of discomfort. But instead, she was grinning at him, her brown eyes shining as his bride gave a happy little laugh.

Lucy removed herself from the position he had put her in to rest her body against the mattress, his seed still coating her buttocks and her inner thighs.

Lucy wrapped her hands around his neck, confidently pulling him down on her. "Let's do it again."

Chapter 9

"WAKE UP."

Christopher winced when he felt something hard hit his cheek. He threw a dirty glare at Steve, who was helping him mend a fence his cattle had broken through, when they had stopped for lunch. Anthony was a few feet away sweet talking the cattle, he had always had a fondness for animals. He was so sweet, Chris hoped life didn't crush him as it often did.

"What's on your mind, married man?" Steve asked sweetly as he bit into an apple. "Is it a certain curly, brown-haired chit? You seem very happy these past few days, did your little mail order bride meet your expectations after all?"

"Talk about Lucy again in that context and I will knock your teeth out," Christopher warned. "For your information, Lucy and I are fine. We've only been married for a few days after all, we're still in wedded bliss."

Steve nodded. "The honeymoon period." He threw away the core of the apple. "I'm happy for you, Chris. Lucy is a sweetheart, way too good for you. I'm already seeing some changes thanks to her."

Christopher furrowed his eyebrows. "Changes?"

"Yes." Steve picked up another apple. He had always liked fruit. "You're less uptight for starters, before Lu everything had to be by the book. Drove us crazy when we were younger. You're even more lenient with the workers. Thank goodness for that, and you smile more. Even before Dad passed you didn't use to smile."

Steve's directness surprised Christopher, he and Lucy had only been married for a few days. He hadn't thought he had changed that much, but perhaps he had. It helped that Lucy was a relaxing person to be with and as compliant and sweet as a newborn kitten. He certainly didn't dread or hate marriage like men his age did.

"Don't get sappy on me," he scoffed instead as he stood up. He wanted to hurry up and get this done so he could go home to his wife. Lucy had promised to bake muffins today, but Christopher wanted to spend some time buried underneath her skirts instead. "Anthony, lunch is over. Let's finish this."

After the brothers finished mending the fence, Christopher headed back home early something he rarely did before, but he supposed being married changed a lot of things for him. His sweet Lucy was pulling out the muffins from the oven when he strolled in, wrapping his arms around her.

"Chris! You're early, dinner isn't finished yet." Christopher interrupted her speech by kissing her until she nearly dropped the muffin pan she was holding.

Lucy returned the kiss eagerly, since their wedding night Lucy had shyly admitted to him that she liked kissing him which resulted in Christopher happily doing it more often. "Afternoon, beautiful." Lucy brightened happily. "I came home early to surprise you." He gave her twelve daisies he had picked up for her earlier. "And to teach you how to feed the chickens."

She followed him to the small chicken coop at the back of the house where the chickens were walking amongst each other as they stared at Lucy and Christopher with beady little eyes. At first she had been afraid to even get the eggs until Christopher showed her a way to distract them.

He took her to where she could find the grain barrel and how to pour water on it to make mush for the chickens. "Are you still afraid of them?" he teased her slightly as they watched the chickens enjoy their food.

"A little. This is the first time I've ever dealt with animals. Mrs. Needles never liked them, though you have to admit chickens are quite different than dogs or cats."

It was the first time she had spoken about her life at the orphanage since her arrival and he couldn't help but look at her curiously. He wanted to know more about it, but he also knew the topic made her uncomfortable and didn't want to push. "How was it growing up at the orphanage?"

"Terrible," she admitted as a chicken nibbled on her shoes. "The orphanage was large, but it was never as nice as this house. It felt like a prison, Mrs. Needles forbade anyone to talk to me. I was terribly lonely."

He pulled her close as he kissed the side of her head. "I'm sorry you had to go through that, precious. Do you feel lonely now? You can be honest with me."

"No," she confirmed as she buried her face in his plaid shirt. "I haven't felt lonely since we married. Especially with you and your family by my side."

"Even Poppy?"

"Even Poppy. What about you, have you ever felt lonely?" She gave him a brittle smile. "You can be surrounded by people and still feel terribly lonely."

He took a deep breath. "Sometimes, when my mother died and later when my father passed. I felt this huge responsibility as the oldest, especially with Iris and Lily being so young. My siblings help me of course, but at the end of the day the responsibility is mine as the oldest."

Lucy squeezed his hand. "It doesn't have to be anymore. You can give me some of the burden, and to your siblings too. We're more than capable of helping you, Chris. You just have to let go."

Christopher kissed her temple before he trailed his lips down to her lips. "I'll work on it, but I don't like giving up control. You know that, Lu."

Lucy huffed. "I can still try. We have our whole life together after all."

They started heading back to the house where Lucy prepared her husband a bath while she finished cooking. There was a knock on the door and when Lucy opened it she saw Finn. "Finn! Come on in, how can I help you? Are you looking for Christopher?"

"He's here?" Finn looked surprised. "He doesn't usually leave his work this early, but then again he's never been married before." He blushed as he murmured an apology. "I actually came to talk with you, Mrs. Bennington. Do you think we could talk outside to get some privacy?"

"Of course. Finn, you don't have to call me, Mrs. Bennington, Lucy is fine."

"Christopher will have my head."

"You call Chris by his first name."

"Well, it's different, we've known each other since we were in the schoolhouse. You're a lady, it's different." Finn removed his hat out of respect once they were outside on the porch. "Please forgive me for bothering you—"

"You're not," she interrupted even though it was rude. "Finn, please tell me what's going on. You're worrying me."

Finn fidgeted as he paced back and forth. "I have a dilemma that I wish to speak to a lady about. I need some advice and as a married lady I suspect you could help me." He turned red. "Please don't repeat this to anyone."

"Of course not."

"I'm in love with your sister-in-law, Poppy," Finn blurted out, nearly ripping his hat in half. "Since the day I laid eyes on her and saw her as a woman, not just the boss's sister. She despises me though. At first, I thought she would come around and she would be open to properly courting, but it's been years and she's as stubborn as a mule. Maybe it's me who can't take the hint and I should just give up instead of discussing it with you."

Lucy thought back to the conversation she'd had with Poppy when she had a nightmare before her wedding and how Poppy had stiffened up at the mere mention of Finn's name. "She's not indifferent, Finn. I think she cares about you, in her own way. Poppy is not a woman who likes to be told what to do. Perhaps she also feels something, but both of you keep going at it the wrong way. Have you told her you wanted to court her?"

"Several times. I brought her flowers, read her poetry, declared my feelings, anything a man can do, but she always says no. I've tried courting other women, but I simply cannot stop thinking about Poppy Bennington. When I do start walking other women home from church or taking them on buggy rides she turns into an absolute hell cat for weeks on end. Her brothers tell me she's a lost cause, an immature brat at her age, but I can't let her go."

"Could it be because you discipline her?" she asked carefully, remembering how he had spanked Poppy on her first day.

He ran a hand through his hair. "I rarely do it and only through her skirts to preserve her modesty. Pop just likes to scream bloody murder. She only gets spanked when she deserves it otherwise she will turn into an insufferable woman."

Lucy patted his arm. "I'm afraid I am not an expert on love or broken hearts. All I can say is do not give up on her, Finn. Poppy is a sweet girl deep down, but also do not feel guilty if you move on. You have the right to your own life."

"I should go." Finn tilted his head in her direction. "Thank you for hearing the woes of a hopeless man."

Lucy nodded, the pity rising in her chest. Love could certainly be a cruel master. Especially an unrequited love. But then again how would the world be if humans could not love?

Chapter 10

STRONG HANDS WERE CLUTCHING her buttocks as Lucy lay on top of her husband. She pressed her hands against his chest to steady herself as she bounced against his cock which was growing inside her even more. They'd been having sex on and off since her husband poked her with his erection at dawn.

Sweat coated her body as she used one hand to play with her erect nipples as Christopher had taught her to do. Meanwhile, Christopher raised his hips to fill her with his member as he panted watching her breasts rise and fall.

Lucy let out a cry when her husband finished inside her as she tumbled against him on the mattress. Her husband pulled her face toward him engulfing her in a deep kiss, his tongue swirled inside her mouth as their tongues fought for dominance with Christopher eventually winning.

He wrapped his strong arms around her as she settled by his side. A kiss landed on top of her head. "You're a fast learner, sweetie."

"I told you it was one of my strengths," she blurted out

before blushing like the virginal bride she had been mere weeks ago. "Do you have to work today?"

"Well, I do run the ranch," he said and chuckled as he kissed her knuckles. "Besides, you have your own chores to do. I could be persuaded to leave early, would you like that, honey?"

She nodded shyly. "I'll bake a cake."

"It's a date." He kissed her forehead before he started getting dressed. "Before I forget, we're going to church tomorrow per Anthony's orders. We have overstayed our honeymoon and Anthony, as a future pastor, is afraid our souls will end up in eternal damnation. To appease his whining, my love, we will play the perfect, pious churchgoers tomorrow." He winked.

The smile fell off her face. Even though she and Christopher had been married for a month she had hardly left their ranch home except when she went to visit her sisters-in-law. She wasn't even sure if people in town, outside of Pastor James, knew they were married.

Lucy touched her short locks. Her hair was curly which meant that even though it had grown it still looked incredibly short. She had been hiding it with a hat or bonnet so far, but even though her head was fully covered you could still tell it was boyish.

What would the townspeople say? She didn't want to embarrass her husband. She then remembered the cruel remark Poppy had made when she saw her hair, would it be the same scenario?

"Lu, honey, is something wrong?" Christopher squeezed her hand while he looked at her with worry.

She hesitated a bit until her husband raised an eyebrow in her direction. "Lu, tell me. We don't keep secrets from each other, remember?"

Lucy nodded obediently as she blurted out, "I'm embarrassed to go to church because of my hair. What if people make fun of me?"

"Then I will gladly break their teeth," he joked as he pinched her button nose. "Kidding aside, I assure you, sweetheart the people of Larkspur Valley are generally nice, you saw how even Poppy came around. Besides, you have many beautiful hats to choose from and I will be by your side every step of the way." He gave her a reassuring kiss, which she returned but she couldn't help, but feel the doubtfulness settling in her chest.

The next day, after breakfast, they left for the ten o'clock service dressed in their Sunday best. Lucy was so nervous even her husband was perplexed as she burnt the toast and misbuttoned her shoes.

"It will be all right, Lu. Don't fret," he reassured her soothingly as they drove into town. "We'll go listen to the service, say a few hellos, and spend the rest of the afternoon with the girls and my brothers."

She nodded, forcing a smile on her face as she stuffed her clammy hands into her cream-colored gloves with the bows at the wrist. Christopher was right, she couldn't avoid church and hide at the ranch forever, but Lucy had never liked meeting new people and she knew how women could sometimes be as vicious as men.

Larkspur Valley Presbyterian Church was a beautiful white building with large windows to let the sunlight in. A golden church bell adorned the top of the church as an elderly Pastor James and his wife greeted the townsfolk.

The church was packed as it seemed the entire town had headed into the service. Lily, dressed in a pink dress, waved to her eagerly from the wagon Hugh was driving. Lucy smiled, at least someone was happy to see her.

Christopher scooped her up in his arms as he helped her down from the wagon. Both of them entered the church with

Lucy nearly gripping his arm. She wished her wedding ring was visible, but it was hidden underneath her glove.

"Chris, how many people know we're married?" she whispered.

He furrowed his brows. "A couple. While I didn't announce it, I do have six meddling, gossipy siblings so I'm sure half the town knows. Why?"

She shook her head, cutting the conversation short once they entered the church. The Benningtons were well known in town as their great-grandfather had been one of the town's original founders when he migrated from Montana to Wyoming. So, Lucy shouldn't be surprised Christopher and his very large family were being stared at, however this time they didn't seem to be staring at Christopher, they were staring straight at her.

The men had funny expressions on their faces as if they were trying not to laugh as they tipped their heads at her in greeting while she forced a smile back. The women around Lucy's age and their mothers exchanged looks of confusion, horror, and anger which made Lucy want to run in the opposite direction.

Thankfully, they slipped into one of the pews toward the front with the rest of the Bennington siblings and Lucy couldn't actually believe she was glad to be sitting next to Poppy.

Pastor James cracked his Bible open, smiling at Lucy and Christopher. "Good morning, brothers and sisters of Larkspur Valley. Before I begin today's service I would like to start off by congratulating one of our dear members, Christopher Bennington who recently got married to Mrs. Lucille Bennington. Mr. and Mrs. Bennington, the congregation and I wish you a long, healthy marriage and may you be blessed in the eyes of our Lord."

Lucy nodded her thanks trying to ignore the gasps and

whispers underneath the lukewarm applause. The rest of the service passed without incident, Lucy was hoping they could scramble out of the church as soon as the service was over, but Christopher simply kissed her forehead and told her there were some things he needed to discuss with Pastor James and Anthony.

"Be a good girl and wait here," he ordered as he brushed a finger against the rapidly burning cheek.

Once he was gone, Lucy looked around to see if she could cling to any of her in-laws, but Hugh was exchanging words with the former town doctor, Steve was joking with the butcher, Iris was giggling with a schoolfriend, and Lily was being teased by Finn while Poppy stood near them frowning, leaving her alone.

Lucy clutched her dainty drawstring purse while she looked at her shoes. She had been halfway through singing a church hymn underneath her breath when she heard the whispers and snickers behind her.

"Mama told me Mr. Bennington dragged her from some shabby, muddy little town west from here. She got herself in the family way to force him to marry her and take her away from her shack."

"But Chrissy, she doesn't look like she's having a baby. She so skinny, almost sickly. Maybe she was faking it?"

"It wouldn't surprise me if she did, what do you think about the newest member of our congregation, Ruth?"

"She's ugly." Ruth let out a squawk like a chicken. "Why would someone as handsome as Christopher marry her? Look at her, she's nearly bald!"

"I heard she cut off all her hair because of lice. She's poor and dirty."

"She looks like a boy. Not pretty or feminine at all, poor Mr. Bennington, to be saddled with a girl like that."

Lucy's ears burned. She couldn't even see in front of her

because of how the tears had plagued her eyes. Her throat felt dry, as if it had stopped functioning, but even if it did work she was too shy to stand up for herself.

So, instead, Lucy did what she knew best. Take the verbal attacks before discreetly making her way outside. She found a quiet place near the fountain of an angel. Lucy crawled next to it as her body quivered with her sobs.

The words the women had said were burning in her head. They were right. She was a poor, trashy woman born out of wedlock who couldn't even spell her name who dared to marry outside her status.

She felt warm hands cup her face as they eagerly wiped away the tears. Christopher was bending down near her, his eyes deep with concern. "Lu, honey, what's wrong? Poppy told me you were upset, something about the ladies not being very kind."

"They hate me." Her voice broke, not daring to look at him. "They hate me for marrying you. They think I'm ugly and skinny, maybe I should buy a wig with my pin money—"

"Lu, look at me." Christopher grabbed her chin firmly to make sure the brunette stared at his blue eyes. "You do not need a wig. I think you're beautiful which is all that matters. Those girls and their vapid words can go straight to Hell for all I care. I married you because I wanted to marry you. Not because anyone forced me."

"They seemed so angry."

"They're angry because I wouldn't marry them. Many of them wanted to marry into money." He helped her up and had her blow her nose into his hankie.

"But didn't I do the same thing? I was looking for financial security when I came here."

"You were simply looking for a warm bed, food, and a roof over your head," he corrected as he led her back to the wagon while he wrapped his arm around her. "You sacrificed your hair to pay for this journey. You left your life in Boston for a chance to start over with me. You've sacrificed enough in your young life, so allow me to spoil you, Lucy Bennington. You deserve the title of Mrs. Bennington not them."

Christopher kissed her firmly, despite the fact they were outside the church, as if he wanted to kiss her sadness away. Reassurance settled into her body at his words. Her own husband thought she deserved to be happy after a miserable life, so why did Lucy feel like she couldn't quite reach the peace he was hoping for her?

"If any of those girls bother you again, let me know." He started driving back toward the house. "All of them have husbands or fathers who can take care of their venomous tongues."

"Oh, Chris, it's not necessary."

"It is. If they hurt my wife I will not stand idly by."

Lucy knew she was not going to change his mind, the Benningtons were a stubborn lot, especially her lovable husband. She squeezed his rough, large hand as she caressed his wedding ring, how had she survived without him for so long?

After that disastrous Sunday, the women of Larkspur Valley, who were enraged they did not snag up the oldest Bennington sibling, left her alone. At least they did not say cruel remarks to her face which is all Lucy could hope for at this point. She very much doubted she would make friends in this town which was all right with her since she was used to not having many friends.

She wasn't quite sure who had put a stop to it, perhaps her husband or Steve who were the most likely suspects, though Lily had whispered to her at bedtime that Poppy had threatened to break Chrissy Simon's nose if she spoke bad about Lucy or her family again. Something which made Lucy smile. Still, she didn't spend more time at church than she had to, though that might change when her brother-in-law finished his education.

The August sun was hot while the air was dry causing her brown curls to stick to her forehead as she rearranged the ribbon of her straw hat. It was Saturday which was one of the rare days Christopher took a half day off to run errands. He had brought her along and while he was at the sawmill she excused herself to go to the mercantile to buy new cloth to make sheets as she and her husband practically soiled them with their juices every night.

Lucy was about to cross the street when she heard Steve calling her, his gold sheriff badge shining against his dark brown vest. "Lu, I went to the post office this morning. You saved me a trip." He handed her a rough looking envelope with coffee stains.

She took the letter, confusion plainly written on her face. She wasn't close to anyone who would write her letters, except perhaps Mrs. Ross, but how would she know she had ended up in Larkspur Valley? Even if she had ,she knew Lucy could not read.

Lucy was about to ask Steve to read the return address to her, but the sheriff seemed distracted by a tiny woman with golden hair who was exiting the town's brothel at the edge of town. Steve mumbled an excuse and left his sister-in-law without another word.

She took in a deep breath as she stared at the letter. What on earth could it be about? Who had sent it?

Chapter 11

I CAN'T UNDERSTAND IT.

Lucy's cheeks flushed red as tears threatened to pour from her eyes as she looked at the letter written with words cut out from several newspaper articles in order for the handwriting not to be recognizable.

It didn't matter how much she looked at the letter, she didn't understand the content. At that moment Lucy grew angry at herself for not having the ability to read even a little. Why must she be so stupid never to have grasped the concept of reading or at least fought hard enough to learn? She then cursed Mrs. Needles, cursing at people was something she rarely did, for being a cruel person who had denied her the basics to survive in this world.

There were very few people in this world who knew Lucy didn't know how to read or write. It was a shameful secret Lucy hardly allowed herself to admit out loud. The only ones who knew were Mrs. Needles, Mrs. Ross, and the Benningtons and the latter would never utter a word out of respect for her privacy.

Twice Christopher had offered to teach her, but she was

too embarrassed to accept his help, besides Christopher often came home so exhausted that she didn't want to burden him by asking him to play the role of husband, rancher, and teacher.

As she walked back to where Christopher's wagon was waiting for her she thought of who could read the letter to her. She didn't have any close friends or family and the letter written from newspaper clippings seemed threatening to her even if she had no idea what it was saying.

She didn't have the guts to ask her husband for fear it was something bad, her brothers-in-law would surely tattle to Christopher about whatever it was along with Finn. Even though Poppy and she were getting along better, the blonde could still be selfish so she was out and Lily was much too young. It only left one person. Iris.

The middle Bennington was kind, knowledgeable, and wise beyond her years even though she was only fifteen. She was also trustworthy. If anyone could help her it was Iris. After Christopher came back with his purchases she begged him to drop her off at his sisters' home, promising to walk back home before it became dark.

She found Iris working on her arithmetic homework as she nervously chewed on her blonde braid. Iris took school-work very seriously as she wanted to earn her teaching certificate even though her elder brothers had told her they would happily provide for her and she didn't have the neces-sity to work.

Iris looked up when she saw Lucy staring at her with a pained expression on her face. "Oh, Lu, what's wrong? Did something happen with Christopher?"

"No." She looked around to search for the other girls. "Where are Poppy and Lily?"

"Poppy is with Hugh, she's helping him pick furniture for

his new bachelor lodgings and Anthony took Lily for a horse-back ride. Now tell me what's the matter?"

Lucy gulped as she gripped the letter in her hand. She knew she was involving Iris in potentially something dangerous that she should let her husband deal with in the first place, but she couldn't stop herself. Christopher had already dealt with enough when he had agreed to marry her on such short notice. She had to take care of this on her own no matter how dangerous.

"I've received a letter." She licked her lips. "However, I do not know how to read. Would you mind reading it to me?"

"Of course." Iris took the letter from her hand. Her blue eyes went wide as she turned to look at her. "It's a threatening letter. Is this a joke?"

"No, it was sent to me. Please tell me what it says. Don't leave one thing out."

"It says, *I know what you did. You'll pay back every penny if it's the last thing you do.* ' What do they mean by that Lucy?"

Perhaps it was the fear or the anxiousness she was feeling, but she found herself spilling the details about her terrible journey out west and the money she stole from Thatcher Watts. "It must be him who's sending the letter, right? I didn't steal from Mrs. Needles and she doesn't care enough to threaten me all the way from Boston. But Thatcher was supposed to head out to California, what is he doing in Larkspur Valley?"

"I don't know, Lucy." Iris bit her lower lip as she looked at her with big blue eyes. "But you need to tell Chris, or Steve since he's the sheriff, about this letter. I don't want you getting hurt, Lucy."

"No!" she nearly screamed. "Christopher or Steve cannot know about this. Swear to me, Iris that you will not let either of them know. I will take care of it."

Iris looked uncomfortable, but nodded.

She breathed a sigh of relief as she smoothed down her skirt. "I need to go home, otherwise Chris will worry."

"Lu, I don't think keeping things from Chris is a good idea. He doesn't like being kept in the dark, but you know best," Iris said slowly. "If you want to—if you're willing—I would be happy to teach you to read and write in the afternoons after morning chores are done. Reading is such an important skill."

Lucy kissed Iris's cheek. "I would like that. Thank you for being such a sweetheart, Iris and for keeping my secret."

When she returned home, Christopher asked her if she would like a change of scenery and have a picnic. She quickly packed some cold sandwiches, a jug of milk, and apples and her husband placed her on top of his large horse so they didn't have to take the wagon.

She found it charming how he managed to grip the reins with one hand while he grabbed the basket with the other. The place he took her was deserted, in a field of larkspur flowers which had inspired the name of the town. After quickly eating the early dinner, Christopher motioned to her to lie on her back on the checkered blanket as they stared at the funny looking clouds.

He stroke her hair as she pointed to a cloud which she claimed was a rabbit, but he said it looked more like a duck.

"My father used to take us here when me and the rest of the kids were little." He closed his eyes. "We would go fishing at a nearby lake, then Mother would be waiting for us with lunch. The last time we came here, Mother was pregnant with Lily. After she passed, Father couldn't bear to take us here anymore. This is the first time I've been here since Lily was born."

Lucy felt her throat tighten as she heard Christopher speak about his parents, she selfishly wished she could have met her own instead of being raised in an orphanage. "What a beautiful memory. I'm sorry about the loss of your parents, Chris. I wish I could have met them."

A twitch of a smile appeared on his face as he stroked her cheek. "They would have loved you. Father always worried I would remain alone. I'm glad to have been able to prove him wrong."

"Well, I did propose to you," she teased him lightly as he started playing with her breasts. "I didn't leave you much of a choice."

"I'm glad you cornered me, Mrs. Bennington, otherwise I would have been married to Chrissy Simon by now." He started unbuttoning her rust-colored dress exposing her underthings. With his quick, able hands he managed to free her breasts from the tight constraint of her corset.

The petite, milky white breasts were exposed to the hot sun the pink nipples already pebbled with desire. Her chest heaved up and down as she scolded him, "Christopher, are you insane? We're in public! Someone could see."

He chuckled as he started pinching her nipples making them turn a darker pink shade. "We're miles away, Lu. Besides if someone even catches a glimpse of you I will tear their eyeballs out." He bit on the sensitive buds with his teeth. A moan escaped her lips as she felt his sharp teeth against the sensitive skin. "Now relax, I want to toy with these pink darlings and as my lawfully wedded wife you are going to let me."

Lucy whimpered with need as he started sucking on her breast, his tongue swirling around the bud as he soothed it with his tongue before biting on it. Hard. Only to soothe the punished skin with his mouth.

She wanted to protest that they should go back home to make love, but she liked her breasts being suckled too much to tell him. She parted her legs as she felt the dewiness start to settle on her quim by the attention he was giving to her breasts.

Christopher's hands roamed around her entire body from the back of her thighs to her waist, and finally her neck while he continued alternating between kissing her breasts and punishing them with his teeth.

His hands gripped the front of her dress before roughly pulling it apart to expose more of her nakedness. She heard the cloth rip while some stray buttons flew in the opposite direction. "Christopher!" she hissed as he started removing her chemise and corset with the same equal strength not caring if he took her home half-naked. "That was a brand-new dress."

"I will buy you a new one." He grinned at her as he stopped playing with her chest for a moment to engulf her in a kiss. "This is the first time I've ever seen you angry. I didn't think it would happen over a dress. Don't worry, sweet pea, you can buy as many dresses as your little heart desires."

Lucy blushed and mumbled something about how he can't keep destroying her clothes on a pure whim.

"Besides a torn dress or two is worth it to see you like this, don't you think?" His hand went underneath her skirt, parted her drawers open, and dipped one finger inside her moist cunny. "You're so wet for me, Lu. Do you want me as much as I want you?"

Lucy could see his hard erection throbbing painfully in his trousers while she saw his glistening muscles peeking from his plaid work shirt. She suddenly didn't care about who walked up on them. Lucy just wanted to feel her husband on top of her.

She nodded, biting her lip as he used one hand to stroke her breast while the other remained underneath her skirt, parting her love lips opened. "Is that a yes? Use your words, Lucy. Do you want me to make love to you?"

Lucy felt her entire body grow warm, but she wasn't so sure if it was because of embarrassment or because her husband was playing with her pussy. "Yes, I want you to. Please."

He let out a low chuckle. "Good girl."

Christopher kept one finger inside her while his thumb caressed her clit which was quickly swelling under its hood. Lucy arched her back, moaning, wanting to feel every inch of his fingers. Her clothes lay forgotten on the grassy fields as she writhed around naked under her husband's toying fingers.

Her fingers caressed her swollen nipples as she thrust her hips into the empty air while her husband's hand continued buried underneath the brown curls. Lucy was whimpering now as she continued staring at his cock still hidden in his trousers. He had unbuttoned some of the remaining buttons of his shirt exposing the dark chest hair.

"Please." She moaned as he pinched her clit sending electric waves down her spine. "Please fill me, Chris. Please."

He chuckled as he planted a chaste kiss on her bottom lip which had grown red from the biting. "I love when you ask nicely, beautiful girl."

Christopher freed his cock from his trousers, exposing his dark red, pulsing erection with the swollen veins. He gripped her hips as he pushed himself into her with ferocity instead of the usual gentleness.

Lucy started moaning as she buried her nails against his shoulders before trailing her fingernails against his back as she felt him thrust inside her. She wrapped her legs around his torso to allow him more space to move freely as he continued to bury his engorged cock inside her tight quim.

She felt him growing inside her, his manhood throbbing with the need to claim every inch of her. He rotated his hips while he gripped the back of her thighs as she felt the thrusts becoming faster and less gentle. But Lucy didn't mind, she enjoyed the unusual display of roughness when he was usually very gentle with her.

Christopher started squeezing her breasts with each stroke while Lucy felt his balls hit the back of her thighs softly. He groaned her name. "Lucy."

Lucy's body trembled as she blurted out, "I know. Me too."

He let out a groan as he spent himself inside of her while Lucy felt her whole body shaking from the orgasm he provided. She was still trying to get used to the orgasmic feeling which resulted after their lovemaking. She felt warm, happy, satisfied, and tired at all once. Lucy couldn't put it into words exactly, but it was a wonderful, dreamy feeling and the only thing stopping her from asking for it four times a day was because her husband was busy herding cattle and breaking in horses.

Christopher dropped next to her burying his lips against her brown curls, "Good girl, Lucy."

Lucy buried her face in the crook of his neck smelling his sweet, woodsy smell. She wished she had never gotten that mysterious letter because it now meant she had to take matters into her own hands.

Chapter 12

WHEN LILY EXPRESSED interest in learning how to bake a cake for Anthony, who was returning to Laramie in exactly two weeks, at the end of August to complete his studies, Lucy had offered to teach her.

Lucy offered to pick up her eleven-year-old sister-in-law the following Saturday since Iris and Poppy would be spending the rest of the day deep cleaning the house to prepare for fall. She felt the soft grass touched her skirts and the hot August sun over her head which made her wonder how Christmases in Wyoming would be.

She flinched when she heard a wail coming from the second Bennington home and she picked up her skirt to run across the field as fast as she could, not caring her hat was removed by how hard she was running.

What happened? Had the person who sent the letter attacked the girls even though Anthony and Hugh were currently staying there? Wetness started to pool in her eyes, if something happened to Iris, Lily, or Poppy she would never forgive herself.

Lucy stopped running when she finally saw the scene in

front of her as perspiration clung to her armpits and neck. Iris, Anthony, Poppy, and Lily were outside near the chicken coop. Poppy was comforting a crying Lily in a motherly way while Anthony and Iris exchanged whispers.

Her brown eyes traveled to the scene Lily was crying over. Three of the Bennington's chickens were outside the coop with their heads chopped off. Their plump bodies were resting next to their heads while blood covered the once green grass.

Lily started wailing even harder when she saw Lucy as she rushed towards her. Her blue eyes were frightened. "Oh, Lucy someone killed Patty, Patsy, and Piper. Why would they do that? Who would be so cruel as to kill innocent chickens?"

Lily balled her hands against Lucy's green dress before burying her face against the material and sobbing.

Poppy threw her an apologetic glance. "She's been like that all morning. I told her it's more than likely a stupid prank. School is still out and you have bored children running around with idle hands."

Iris shared a nervous look with Lucy. "We live too far from town and other farms for children to play pranks on us, no matter how bored they are. Besides, they know Hugh and Anthony are staying with us."

Anthony ran a hand through his dark hair as he inspected the dead chickens. "I agree with Iris, besides for a child's prank this seems a tad too violent. Lucy, what's wrong?"

Lucy hadn't realized it, but she had started crying as she continued staring at the chickens. *It's my fault, it's all my fault. I shouldn't have stolen the money no matter how desperate I was.*

Poppy looked annoyed. "Oh, no. Not you, too. You're as sensitive as Lily. Dead chickens are not the worst thing you'll see growing up as a rancher's wife. How are you going to make it during butchering season? Hugh, Steve, and Christopher kill at least five pigs for the winter."

This caused Lucy to cry harder.

Anthony groaned. "Pop, you are as helpful as a hurricane. I'm going to go find Chris. Iris, keep an eye on Lucy and Lily. Poppy, please don't make Iris cry, too."

Poppy scowled.

Thirty minutes later, Christopher was leading a trembling Lucy back into their house after picking her up from his siblings' home after she had started crying like a child. "You need a nap," he told her as he carried her up the stairs before leading her up to their bedroom and plopping her on the bed. He handed her, her white nightgown. "You're overtired."

"I'm not. It's just the chickens, I'm not used to seeing blood." She tried to protest, but she still got dressed in her nightgown then rested her head against the pillows. "I'm sorry I made you come all this way. I know you're preparing for a shipment."

Christopher shook his head. "You're my wife. You never have to apologize for needing me. Now spread your legs and show me your sweet little pussy."

She turned red. "Why?"

"Just spread them, Lucy like a good girl. A good orgasm will tire you out."

She hesitated a bit, but eventually did as she was told. Three seconds later, she started hollering like a mad woman when she realized her husband was lowering his mouth down there instead of pulling his cock out like she had expected. "What are you doing?" her shoulders shook. "It's not proper."

"It's perfectly normal behavior between a husband and wife. Now relax, Lu." He spread her legs calmly as if she hadn't spoken. He then used his tongue to lick every nook and cranny of her womanhood.

She whimpered a bit as she felt his hot tongue in her more private parts which only fingers had touched before. Her toes curled as he sucked on her plump folds, taking them fully into his mouth as he nibbled on the sensitive flesh gently.

"Oh, oh." No words came out, only sounds, as her fingers gripped the pillows. Lucy felt Christopher's tongue spread her lower lips apart. He darted the thick muscle in and out of her as he used both hands to keep her thighs wide open while her nightgown wrapped itself over her belly.

He squeezed three orgasms out of her with just his tongue and if anyone would have passed by them, they would have thought she was being murdered. Shivers spread through her entire body as she tried to calm down her beating heart. She could feel her aching pussy covered with a mixture of her juices and his saliva.

Christopher wiped his mouth with the back of his hand before he kissed her forehead. "I have to get back to work for a few more hours. Try to get some rest. Don't overwork your-self with dinner. A simple sandwich will do."

Lucy nodded, still feeling very dazed about what just happened, and secretly wondering how she could get her husband to pleasure her like that more often.

She must have fallen asleep because when she opened her eyes again, the clock on her nightstand read four in the afternoon. Lucy quickly got up and got dressed otherwise she would never get dinner done at this rate. The headless chickens thankfully were the last thing on her mind at the moment.

The mistress of the house had been busy cutting up vegetables when she heard a knock on the door. She cleaned her hands on her apron and went to answer the door. Then she wished she never had.

Standing in front of her was the man who had spent years working at the orphanage where she had grown up. The man who would sneer at her every time Mrs. Needles scolded her for working too slow. The man she had stolen one-hundred dollars from out of desperation. Thatcher.

He looked worse for wear, but then again she had to remind herself he had spent most of the time being an alcoholic. He was still tall with a shaggy white beard wearing a dirty vest and brown pants. Thatcher was in his later forties, but physically he looked just as strong as Steve or Christopher.

Thatcher grinned at her showcasing a row of yellow teeth. "I finally found you, girly. Had to wait for that annoying husband of yours to leave. He follows you everywhere doesn't he?" he stared at her engagement ring and wedding band. "Nice rings."

Lucy hid her hand behind her back and said weakly, "You are supposed to be in California."

"I was, but I seem to be missing some money. A hundred dollars if I recall correctly, though now that you mentioned it, it might have been a thousand—"

"It was a hundred." She gripped the doorway. "I'm sorry, but the journey was long and I ran out of money. Have you been following me?"

Thatcher nodded as he spat on the ground. "Wasn't easy especially when the Benningtons breed like rabbits."

"And the letter? The chickens with their heads cut off?"

"All me. Straight out of a crime novel." The grin he had, had quickly disappeared. "Now you and I need to talk, Mrs. Bennington about what you and your little husband are going to do about paying me back and then some. I've wasted too much time chasing after you."

"Then you'll leave me alone?" Lucy looked around in case Finn or Christopher were nearby.

"Sure, sweetheart. Seeing a woman shop and giggle with her family members quickly bores me."

Lucy swallowed, hoping she didn't regret this. "Fine, we'll talk. Not here. I don't want my husband to find us. He cannot know about this." Thatcher nodded. "Lead the way."

Thatcher had come walking, but her legs were not as long or as fast as his and it took them thirty minutes to reach the shack Thatcher was staying in. It was sloppily made of old pieces of wood, and it looked like it was destined to fall at any second.

He led her inside the dirty shack which smelled like urine and manure. "I would offer you tea, but I'm not used to having ladies over." His tone was sarcastic, making fun of her low birth and how just a few months ago she had been nothing but an indentured servant. "I'll make our visit short, Lucy girl. I expect, in a month's time, five-hundred dollars burning a hole in my pocket."

"Five-hundred dollars?" she blurted out. It would be hard enough to get a hundred dollars since she was sure Christopher would not let her work, let alone five-hundred dollars. "But I only stole one-hundred dollars."

"But I wasted too much time searching for you, sweetie. More money down the drain trying to search for your little behind. You understand, don't you?" Thatcher patted her cheek. "Besides you're married to the eldest Bennington, this is just some pocket change for him."

"Christopher can't know about this," she argued weakly. "I'll give you the money. All of it. Just don't tell him." Her husband and the townspeople already knew she was an orphaned, uneducated bastard, no need to add the word thief to it.

"Fine." He didn't seem eager to deal with Christopher

either. "But be warned, Lucy girl, if I don't get my money your littlest sister-in-law will pay. You all love her, don't you? She's a sweet doll would be a shame if her pretty face was ruined."

Lily? Would this bastard dare hurt a little girl? She was only eleven and the first Bennington who had welcomed her with open arms. "If you hurt, Lily, I'll tell the sheriff. He's my brother-in-law."

"Honey, you won't tell your husband, let alone the sheriff. He might be your brother-in-law, but if you start talking about a man, who no one has seen, he might believe there is something wrong with that beautiful head of yours. After all you're the only one whose seen me and no one in this town would dare go after a Bennington." He tapped Lucy's nose. "One month, Lucy and then I better see five-hundred dollars. Understood?"

Lucy couldn't speak. Her mouth felt dry, but she managed to nod. How was she supposed to obtain that much money? She didn't have that much pin money saved!

Thatcher continued staring at her and she suddenly felt itchy. She needed to get out of here. Now. She exited his shack and noticed it was already dark. Wrapping her arms around her body she started hurrying back home, she would never get dinner done at this rate.

About halfway done with her journey she felt herself being pulled by the back of her dress and up on the hard saddle of a horse. Was it Thatcher? Had he decided to finish her once and for all? Lucy shut her eyes and started scratching her kidnapper across his chest.

"Where the hell have you been, Lucy?"

Lucy stopped scratching and opened her eyes; she twisted her head forward wondering if dealing with Thatcher was better than dealing with her husband. With her nails she had unbuttoned his shirt halfway, exposing his chest and he had a confused look on his face sprinkled with annoyance.

Christopher tightened his grip on her as the horse started taking them back home. "Well, little girl, did the cat get your tongue or what?"

"I-I," she squeaked as she stared at his electric blue eyes. There was no way she was going to tell her husband about Thatcher, she would figure out how to get the money come hell or high water. Her husband did not need to know she was a thief. "I went for a walk, and I lost track of time."

He raised a dark eyebrow. "In the dark? So far away from the ranch? After I told you, you shouldn't be running around by yourself or at the very least without letting me know? Lu, you could have gotten killed or kidnapped running around by yourself. Larkspur Valley still has less than pleasant people with bad intentions around."

Don't I know it, Lucy slumped her shoulder at being scolded. "I'm sorry. I didn't think it would be anything to fuss over."

"You're still getting a tanning when we get home."

Lucy gaped as she felt her cheeks coloring with her shame. "Why? I apologized."

"And I appreciate it," he said calmly as he stopped the horse. Christopher stretched his hand, helping her down, first. "I warned you during your first few days here, Lu, not to leave the ranch without telling me where you were going. It worries me and you willingly left without leaving a note, especially in the dark. You broke a rule. You're getting spanked, Lucy, end of story."

Christopher gave her a quick kiss before patting her rump and instructing her to wait in their bedroom for him. Lucy did as she was told, not wanting to make things worse for herself, though she didn't know what was worse, dealing with her husband or with Thatcher.

Lucy had paced around the room exactly ten times before Christopher made his way upstairs. He had a wooden spoon in his hand, Lucy's eyes immediately welled up with tears. Christopher sighed as he sat on the bed and opened his arms to her. "Come here, beautiful."

She immediately flung herself into his arms, her slim body shaking as she buried her face in his chest. "I'm sorry, I won't do it again. Please don't punish me."

He ran a hand through her brown hair. "Sweetheart, you do know I will never beat you like Mrs. Needles did, right? I will only strike your bottom and the back of your thighs to correct your naughtiness. After, all will be forgotten, and we will be able to move on. We will not speak about it anymore. During your wedding vows you promised me your obedience as your husband." He tipped up her chin to make her stare at him. "Are you going to be obedient, my darling Lu?"

She nodded. It was just a spanking. She could take it. Though she hated to disappoint him.

"Good girl. Lay across my lap."

Lucy gently did as she was told, feeling awkward as she did so. She felt nervous as her husband lifted her dress and petticoats over her waist. She stiffened slightly as she felt him untie the ribbons holding her drawers up.

When she felt the cool air on her bottom, Lucy started squirming. Christopher patted her bottom warning her lightly to, "Behave."

Lucy sucked in her breath before nodding, forcing herself to keep still.

"I'm giving you ten slaps with the spoon," he warned her, though his voice was soft. No doubt he didn't want to scare her since Mrs. Needles had used physical punishment as practically a form of torture. "Then you'll be getting into your nightgown, and I will get us something to eat."

"But you don't know how to cook," she blurted out.

A smile tugged on his face. "I was a bachelor before I married you, Lu. Of course, I know how to cook."

Then without another word he slapped down the wooden spoon on her bare bottom. She let out a small squeak as a pink oval shaped circle marked her skin. A second mark soon appeared on the other cheek followed by a third.

Christopher's spanks were slow, precise, and sharp and destined to leave a sore mark in its wake. The smacks didn't hurt exactly, but she would be lying if she didn't feel her bottom getting achy. She felt as the spoon dug into the pale flesh turning it a dark pink.

Lucy's pinkened cheeks wiggled under the administration of the spoon and once or twice, when Christopher delivered a rather sharp smack against the fleshly part of her bottom, she opened her legs showing off her womanly charms her husband knew so well.

Tears burned in her eyes, not because of the pain because her bottom was barely a dark pink and decorated with oval shaped marks, but because she was embarrassed. Partly because she was being spanked as if she were a naughty brat and partly because she hated disappointing Christopher, especially with what was going on with Thatcher.

"Ten." The spoon landed with a final slap against her rear end, digging against the punished skin. He immediately started rubbing the aching skin, even though it didn't hurt much. It mostly stung. She would still be able to sit though probably not very comfortably for the next few days.

Her breathing became shallow as she concentrated on her husband's rough hands rubbing her delicate skin. She couldn't help but notice there was a familiar heat growing in between her legs. Lucy quickly shut her eyes. *Oh, not now,* how could she get sexually frustrated over a discipline spanking?

She silently prayed he didn't dip a finger in between her legs to find the moisture nestled in there.

Much to her relief, Christopher immediately scooped her up in his arms and placed her on his lap with her sore nates dangling over his hard thigh. He immediately kissed her causing her heart to flutter, as he rubbed her back while she tried to avoid her wetness getting on his pants.

"There, honey that wasn't so bad. Was it?" Christopher prompted as she shook her head no. She felt a little sore, but nothing to cry about. She had honestly been expecting worse by how much Poppy had hollered when Finn had spanked her, but Iris had always said her older sister was dramatic.

"Good girl. Now remember to let me know whenever you leave the house. I know the country might appear safe, but there's danger lurking around every corner." He tweaked her nose. "Now get ready for bed while I make us some grilled cheese sandwiches."

Lucy forced a smile on her face, *oh husband, you have no idea how dangerous the country can be.*

Chapter 13

ONE WEEK LATER, after her weekly reading lesson with Iris, Christopher sat her down at the dining room table. She fiddled with her nervous fingers when she looked at his serious face. Had he found out about Thatcher somehow? But that was impossible, she still had three weeks left!

But then again Christopher had Bennington eyes everywhere. Steve was the sheriff, Hugh was working at the medical practice, and Anthony was often in town getting ready to leave Larkspur Valley at the same time Thatcher was due to collect five-hundred dollars.

Lucy's brain hardly had time to think anymore before Christopher placed a notebook, ink jar, pen, and a box filled with money in front of her. Her brown eyes widened as she stared at the green bills. It wasn't five-hundred dollars, but it was still plenty. At least a hundred.

She fought the urge to stuff them in the pocket of her dress and throw them in Thatcher's face.

"Iris tells me you're good at arithmetic." Christopher opened the notebook showing her several columns filled with rows which listed things like *grocery, feed, store, lumber, coal.*

Lucy nodded, but her eyes never left the stack of money. "Mrs. Needles didn't want me to be short on money whenever I did errands, so I became good at counting money."

"Then, my dear wife, you'll be in charge of our monthly bill keeping. You will track our spending, make sure we are not going over budget, and store the money." He'd broken the bills in half. "Half of it you will leave for me to deposit in the bank and make the necessary payments in town and the other half you will deposit in our safe. In my wardrobe there is a fake wall in the closet's back. If you gently push it up, you will find a safe. The combination is our wedding date. You can use my previous notes to help you get started. Do you think you'll be able to do that, Lu?"

Lucy nodded, the excitement bubbling in her chest at the idea her husband was trusting her with such a huge responsibility. "I'll do a good job, I promise. I won't let you down."

Christopher chuckled in amusement. "I know you won't. You're always such a good, sweet girl."

Her smile faltered.

Christopher looked at her with such loving tenderness it made her chest hurt from the guilt she was feeling. He ruffled her brown hair as he gave her a gentle kiss. "I love you, Lucy Bennington."

Lucy let out an unexpected squeak. His declaration of love could not have come at the worst possible moment. She had been waiting for it, hopefully, like any young bride, but she did not want it to be like this when she had all these problems in her head. But it wasn't like she could tell him that.

He frowned. "Are you all right, darlin'? You look flushed."

"I'm blushing." This wasn't a complete lie. She cupped his face in her small hands to pull him forward, so they were nearly touching each other's foreheads. "I love you too."

Christopher grinned at her as he pulled her up from the chair and started spinning her around causing excited giggles to escape from Lucy's lips.

"I have to go meet my workers." Christopher fondled her skirt covered bottom. "I'll see you at dinner."

Lucy bit her lip and nodded. Once he was gone, she slipped up to their bedroom, towards Christopher's wardrobe, and discovered the safe. Her heart was thumping like mad inside her chest, growing even faster the second she saw the large amount of stacked bills.

Her trembling hands took three-hundred dollars and stuffed them in the pocket of her dress. Lucy fought the urge to steal the remaining two-hundred dollars, but it would be too much of a gamble. She was already walking on thin ice as it was.

The money felt heavy in her pocket at the betrayal she had just made. Lucy felt like the world's most horrible wife. Especially since she had stolen from him minutes after he had declared his love for her. But it was either her morals or Lily's life. Besides she would get the remaining two-hundred dollars some other way.

Lucy was almost sure that if Christopher knew what she was going through he would agree with her. At least she hoped so.

If Christopher knew where she currently was, he would probably regret giving her such a light spanking a few days prior. After her husband had left the house after lunch, Lucy found herself going back to Thatcher's shack silently praying she would return before her husband returned otherwise, she would earn another spanking.

Lucy jumped back when Thatcher opened the door with

a cigar dangling from his mouth. His breath smelled like alcohol while his clothes were dirty and clinging to his body due to sweat. "Back already?" He gave her a toothy grin. "You work fast. I should have asked for a thousand."

Lucy Bennington did not consider herself a hateful person, but even she couldn't deny the rage bubbling in her chest and the urge she had to slap Thatcher. She pushed a paper bag forward with the three-hundred dollars she had taken from the safe. "It was all I could spare. That is three times the amount I stole from you. I can't get any more money."

His face darkened. "How much is missing?"

She chewed on her bottom lip. "Two-hundred. I swear there is no way I can get any more money. My husband handles our finances."

Thatcher laughed as he tucked the paper bag inside his ugly coat. "Don't bother lying to me, sweet cheeks. You belong to one of the wealthiest families in this damn town. Two-hundred dollars is nothing to them, especially with all the cattle your dear husband is expected to sell." He reached forward, pulled her arm, and dragged her until they were face to face. "You already screwed me over twice, you stupid brat. You will not do it again. I've already been generous by giving you until the end of the month to come up with the money. Either bring me the money by the end of August or the little Bennington will be joining her poor parents at those pearly gates very soon."

Lucy gasped as she stared at his face, hoping it was just a cruel joke or he was fibbing with her. However, this was the most honest she had seen Thatcher. He really would harm Lily with no hesitation even if she was a child.

Her feet started moving backwards and she almost fell on her behind.

"Do you need a ride back to your grand home, Mrs. Bennington?"

Lucy didn't answer, instead she started to run.

Chapter 14

"IRIS! IRIS! IRIS!"

Iris gave an annoyed sigh as she looked up from the spelling book which she was using to teach Lucy how to sound out words. They had been meeting twice a week during lunch ever since Iris offered her services.

Lucy couldn't help but think that Iris already had the strict teacher persona at only fifteen years old. When she finally got her own classroom, Lucy had no doubt she would rule with an iron fist and plenty of love.

"What is it, Lily? Are you crying again? You're eleven years old, you are much too old to be crying." Poppy was the one who usually babied Lily, but since she had forced Hugh to take her to the dressmaker for a new winter coat, Iris was all Lily had.

Lily's pale face was covered in tears as she carried the body of a doll. The head, arms, and legs were missing, and the body was covered with red paint in the shape of a number one. "Someone took Orchid from my outside play-house. Look what they did to her! They killed her!"

Iris ruffled her little sister's blonde hair looking unsure of how to offer comfort. "Oh, Lily it's probably Hugh playing a prank on you. You know how malicious he can be, and you did break his new pocket watch if you remember."

"It was an accident. Besides Hugh knows Orchid is my favorite doll, he would never do that."

Iris sighed. "We can ask him when he comes back with Poppy. Now, Lil, don't cry, we'll get you a new doll. A prettier one." She turned to Lucy. "Right, Lucy?"

Lucy felt like she was going to vomit. It was Thatcher's doing. He was warning her, she only had one more week to come up with the money otherwise he would harm Lily. She had managed to steal one-hundred dollars more from several members of the Bennington family.

Lucy had visited Steve last week carrying a cherry pie and when he had been busy eating and sharing with his co-workers Lucy had managed to steal fifty dollars from the cashbox he had in his desk drawer which contained paid bail money. Later, she had sneaked into Anthony's bedroom, opened his suitcase, and pulled out twenty dollars from the extra money he was taking back to school. Hugh had been the scariest person she had to steal from. He was always polite to her, but she couldn't help but notice his eyes were shifty and dark much like Poppy's sharp look.

When she had visited him feigning a stomachache, she had taken an old gold pocket watch he hopefully didn't need any more and pawned it off, receiving thirty dollars. This had been over the course of two weeks and Lucy was surprised she wasn't in the middle of a nervous breakdown from stealing from her family when they were slowly welcoming her into their home.

Lucy was a disgusting, selfish, cowardly girl who had no right to wear the Bennington name.

"Lucy, are you all right? You're looking pale. Do I need

to call Chris again? Don't worry, it's paint, not blood. I'm sure it's just the dreadful Hugh's idea of a prank."

"I think you should go into town to get Lily another doll," Lucy blurted out. She needed to get the last of the money and fast. She didn't know what Thatcher was capable of, but after what she witnessed she certainly didn't want to know.

She knew Poppy had several of her late mother's jewels in her jewelry box since the blonde bragged about it often. She supposed she could take one or two and pawn it as she had done to Hugh's pocket watch even if Poppy was scarier than Thatcher. To do so, though, she needed to get everyone out of the house since Anthony, Iris, Lily, and Poppy lived there and she didn't want to run the risk of running into anyone and explaining her shame.

Iris frowned. "Now? But we're in the middle of a lesson. Lily is old enough to live without a doll."

Lily cried harder and stomped her foot while Iris murmured that she was acting like a spoiled little brat.

"Iris, just take her. We can continue our lesson tomorrow." Lucy hated how desperate her voice sounded, she was on the verge of crying just like Lily, but for entirely different reasons. "Lily needs a doll. She's already been through a lot."

"Fine." Iris crossed her arms irritably. "Lily, get your hat and we'll walk over to town. Hopefully, we run into Hugh and Poppy, and they can give us a ride back."

Lucy watched them almost with quiet desperation as Lily and Iris tied the ribbons of their hats underneath their chin and walked to town. Iris had invited Lucy to come along, but Lucy told her she would clean up her schoolbooks and head home.

Once she was sure Iris and Lily were far away from the house, Lucy headed upstairs nearly climbing the stairs two at a time, trying to ignore how her palms were becoming slick with sweat.

Poppy's bedroom was located at the end of the hallway and was the biggest since she was the oldest. It was decorated in shades of green and pink with frills and lace everywhere. It was surprisingly feminine. She didn't know why she had been expecting instruments of torture to be there.

Everything was neat and orderly; Lucy had no trouble finding her jewelry box. If she didn't take Poppy's jewels then Thatcher would kill Lily, but if Poppy found out she was the culprit, then Poppy would end her, not caring at all that she was her brother's wife.

Inside the jewelry box there was beautiful, expensive jewelry belonging to Poppy's grandmother and mother. She looked through the bracelets, rings, and dainty necklaces focusing on which ones would bring the most money.

She finally picked a gold bracelet with several blue stones and a thick ruby necklace, silently praying it would be enough to earn the last one-hundred dollars. Lucy had been about to turn around and run back home when she felt someone gripping her shoulder.

The person turned her around and pushed her harshly against the wall. Lucy gasped when she stared into the angry, foxy blue eyes of Poppy Bennington. The blonde looked close enough to strangle her while her nostrils flared. "What the hell do you think you're doing?" Poppy looked at her jewelry in Lucy's hands and let out a bitter laugh. "You're stealing from me? Why doesn't it surprise me? I told Chris you were nothing but a poor gold digger—"

Lucy prevented her from speaking by placing a hand against her mouth. She narrowed her eyes, but Lucy finally let her go. Lucy wiped her sweaty hand on her skirt, but never let go of the jewels. "I can explain," she promised weakly.

"You have ten seconds," her sister-in-law hissed.

Poppy was no doubt being serious as Lucy started spilling everything about how Mrs. Needles had made her life hell, how the journey had been more expensive than she had anticipated and in a moment of weakness she had stolen from Thatcher, how Thatcher had followed her and was now demanding five-hundred dollars or he would kill Lily, and lastly how she had been stealing from her family for weeks.

Once she finished her story, Poppy looked less angry, but she still snatched the jewels from her hand. "You're an idiot. You should have told Steve the second this Thatcher showed up causing problems." She paused. "But I understand it's a pride thing. Women might not have much in this male dominated world, but they do have their pride."

"I'm so sorry, Poppy," Lucy whispered. "I shouldn't have done all of this. You shouldn't pay for my mistakes, but I got nervous and desperate. Now I've harmed everyone and made this worse. I really am sorry. I've been a lousy sister-in-law."

"I'm just glad you're not this somber, perfect little mouse everyone keeps gushing over." Poppy ignored her apology as she pulled out a wooden box with engraved poppy flowers from under her bed and pulled out a pistol. "I'm going to help you take care of this."

Lucy's brown eyes widened as she stared at the pistol. She had seen her husband and Steve carry one, but she had never actually touched one while Poppy seemed completely at ease with it. "Shouldn't we tell Steve?"

"No. He and Christopher will just give him the money to shut him up. But it would just encourage him to keep popping up every few months asking for more before he poisons your reputation in town." Poppy started loading the pistol calmly as if she were sewing. "If we want to scare the little vermin off for good, we have to play with him a little. Like a cat does to a mouse. You're not giving him a cent after we're done with him, he will be thanking his lucky stars we let him go with a warning."

Lucy shifted nervously, silently thinking it would have been better if Poppy had just strangled her. "Shouldn't we at least let Finn or Hugh know?"

Poppy scowled at her. "We do not need a man. You and I are perfectly capable of taking care of a low born like Thatcher. Now tell me where he lives, and we'll take care of this before dinner."

Lucy hesitated. "Why are you helping me?"

Poppy blinked her beautiful blue eyes reminding her of a doll. "Because you are my brother's wife, my sister-in-law. You're family. Families help each other clean up their messes. Now stop whining and tell me where Thatcher lives."

____

Chapter 15

____

"I DON'T THINK we should do this, Poppy."

Lucy might as well be speaking to a blank wall because Poppy was headed to Thatcher's shack like her life depended on it. She knew the gun was safely hidden in Poppy's dress pocket and she couldn't help but curse herself out. She should have just told Christopher about Thatcher, at least he was more levelheaded than Poppy.

"Don't be a scaredy cat, Lucy. You have already avoided this long enough. We need to take care of this Thatcher before you really become a thief."

Lucy's cheeks burned, but she didn't say anything as Poppy went to Thatcher's home and pulled the door open without even bothering to knock.

Thatcher was in his equally drunk state from when Lucy came begging him earlier. He was wearing the same dirty clothes and from the look of it he'd spent whatever money he had on cheap liquor while he waited for Lucy to deliver the last two-hundred dollars.

"Lucy girl, you made it. Right on time!" By some form of miracle, he managed to stand up on clumsy legs. He stared at Poppy lewdly. "And you brought your sister-in-law, how sweet. Piper, right?"

"Poppy," the blonde responded coolly.

Thatcher quickly lost interest as he turned back to look at Lucy. There was greed hinting in his eyes. "You have the rest of the money for me, Lucy girl?"

Lucy opened her mouth to speak, but no words came out. Poppy had bullied her into leaving the money behind, no doubt knowing that as soon as Lucy saw Thatcher she would cave. "I'm not giving you the money." She didn't know how she managed to say the words without bursting into tears.

Thatcher stared at her long and hard before he cracked his neck, then he showcased his ugly yellow teeth. "Then I suppose you don't care about what happens to poor Lily—"

Before Lucy could even protest, Poppy had body slammed Thatcher against the wall. Even though Poppy was significantly smaller, Thatcher was still heavily drunk. Poppy was now pressing the gun against his chin with a crazy look in her eye.

Her nails were digging against Thatcher's flabby neck and Lucy had to admire her courage, no wonder all her brothers joked around that she could probably do a better job at being the town sheriff.

Poppy might be mean, vindictive, and less than friendly but she had been forced into the "mother" role at just fourteen and had been a mother figure to Anthony, Iris, and especially Lily and a companion to their father when he had been alive. Like Christopher she was the glue that held the Bennington family together.

If there was one thing Lucy knew about Poppy was that she defended her family with her bare hands. Even Poppy had grudgingly accepted Lucy as family when she defended her against those women who had laughed about her hair at church and right now, she was risking her life to clean up one of Lucy's messes.

Poppy pressed the gun tightly against his chin. "If you ever threaten my baby sister again, I will remove your eyeballs from your eye sockets." She handled the gun with ease as she tightened her hold against Thatcher's chest. "Thatcher, you will forget about the money and about hurting Lily or Lucy unless you want to deal with my brother, the sheriff. You have two hours to leave Larkspur Valley for good. If I see you around town like a slimy cockroach, I will not hesitate to put a bullet through your skull even if there is a lack of a brain."

For Poppy's sake, she didn't want to see her sister-in-law hanged, she hoped she was just bluffing. But Poppy had that terrifying look in her eye which let Thatcher know she was dead serious.

Thatcher's own hand flew out as he gripped Poppy's own chest hard. Poppy gasped, being caught by surprise as she staggered on her feet, dropping the gun. Thatcher easily scooped it up in his hand as he raised his foot, kicking Poppy harshly in the belly causing her to fall on the ground.

Poppy let out a low cry, her blue eyes widened in fear when Thatcher pressed the gun against her forehead. "No one threatens me, little bitch. If someone's head is going to be blown off, it's going to be yours." He grinned at her. "Not to worry, I will give you a wonderful parting memory."

The blonde spit on his face as he reached over to raise her skirt. Thatcher cursed at her, slapping her down.

Lucy stood frozen with fear in the corner as she stared at the scene in front of her. She had to do something otherwise Poppy would be killed. With trembling hands, she gripped the neck of a beer bottle which stood on the table behind her as she silently approached Thatcher.

Don't be a coward, she scolded herself. Everyone thought

she was a frightened, weak little thing: Thatcher, Christopher, Poppy. She wanted to prove them wrong, she needed to prove them wrong if Poppy was going to survive.

Before she lost her nerve, she slammed the beer bottle against his head. Thatcher hollered, dropping the gun as pieces of glass fell on the floor, blood poured down his forehead. Poppy used the opportunity to snatch the fallen gun and shoot Thatcher three times, one bullet in each leg and one bullet in his shoulder.

Poppy seemed determined to finish him off, but Lucy grabbed her shoulder. "Let's go and get Steve. Let him finish him off."

Poppy curled her lip. "He will get away."

"He won't be able to leave without spilling blood." Lucy tugged on her arm. "If you continue doing this you will kill him and not even Steve will be able to save you once you interfere with the law."

"He threatened Lily and you. This scum will continue doing it unless we stop him."

"Poppy, please. You're not thinking straight, I am. Let's get Steve so we can put an end to this."

Blue eyes met brown and finally Poppy grudgingly agreed as she took Lucy's hand. "Fine." The two girls started running towards town leaving a moaning Thatcher behind as he cradled his injured legs.

It took almost an hour to reach town usually, but Poppy and Lucy were running so fast they made it in thirty minutes. Steve nearly jumped out of his seat when they barged into the sheriff's office.

He stood up abruptly as he looked at his sister and Lucy's disheveled clothing and their flushed faces. Steve's blue eyes widened as he looked at Poppy's hand which was still holding the gun. "Who the hell did you kill?"

Chapter 16

"WHAT ON EARTH was going through your heads, girls?"

Steve let out an exhausted sigh as he served himself a drink. It was nearly nine in the evening, and everyone was exhausted. Hugh was with Thatcher taking care of his bullet wounds and according to him not being the least bit gentle. He was proud of his twin for her quick thinking even though Christopher and Steve were upset about how everything came to be. Thatcher was due to be sent to the state penitentiary, after his wounds healed, to serve a long-term sentence for extortion, threat to commit murder, and for harming a female.

Anthony was set to leave town tomorrow, but tonight he was keeping an eye on Iris and Lily. As for Poppy there was no doubt she was nursing a very sore, red bottom. Finn and Chris had come scrambling to the second Bennington home as soon as they were informed about what happened.

As soon as Finn had made sure she was healthy he had dragged her upstairs to whip her "defiant, aggressive little ass." Poppy had protested of course, but Finn was stronger than she and her brothers were too angry at both her and

Lucy for their recklessness that they didn't try to defend her too much.

Lucy squirmed as she looked nervously in her husband's direction. While Steve had raged on and yelled at both his sister and sister-in-law, Christopher had remained quiet. Somehow his silence was worse than his scolding.

He had hardly raised an eyebrow when she told them about all the money she had stolen from the family and how she and Poppy had foolishly gone in search of Thatcher. Lucy wiped her sweaty palms on her dress. She wished he would say something to her. Even screaming and scolding was acceptable.

"I'm sorry," Lucy responded meekly. "We shouldn't have gone to see Thatcher. I should have told you about him as soon as he threatened Lily and when he started leaving all those clues behind. I will return every cent I stole, I promise—"

"It's not about the money, Lucy." Steve ran a hand through his inky black hair. "You and Poppy acted without thinking. You are lucky your foolish heads weren't blown off."

Lucy blushed and stared at her lap. How was she supposed to respond to that?

Christopher stood up and squeezed her shoulder. "Steve, Lucy is exhausted. We can talk about this tomorrow."

"Fine." Steve didn't look pleased by the idea. Before he left, Lucy handed him a small sack which contained the money she had stolen, including the money she received when she had pawned Hugh's pocket watch. "Try not to get yourself killed before breakfast, Lu, and never listen to Poppy again."

"I think Poppy was very brave," Lucy spoke up. "She just wanted to protect her family. Either of you would have done the same thing."

Steve rolled his eyes but didn't argue with her.

Lucy flinched when the door closed behind him, leaving Lucy alone with her husband. She couldn't bear to look at him, she was full of shame and guilt about everything she had put him through in the short months of their marriage. Lucy shut her eyes tightly.

"Lucy, look at me."

His voice was gentle and soft. He didn't sound angry, more like hurt.

"Lucy. Look. At. Me."

Christopher's voice had grown sharper, almost scolding. Lucy opened her brown eyes to see Christopher kneeling in front of her squeezing her hands together. He stared at her with vivid blue eyes, and she wanted to do nothing but engulf him with kisses and apologize for being such a pain in the butt.

"Have I been a bad husband?"

The question caught her by surprise. That was the last thing she thought he would say. Quite the contrary Christopher had been a kind, patient husband, especially since she ruined everything she touched. Not to mention he had married her after they had exchanged only one letter. Chris was protective, kind, and loving. Even when he made love to her, he was tender and gentle.

"N-No, of course not! You've been a perfect husband. Why would you ask that, Chris?"

"Because you didn't trust me." His voice was almost accusing. "You never mentioned Thatcher, or the threats he made against you, which I could have easily taken care of. I thought our marriage was filled with trust and we could tell each other everything. Now that I know you've been hiding this secret behind my back, I'm not sure—"

"Of course, I trust you, Christopher!" Lucy blurted out as she pulled him in for a tight hug. The tears were streaming down her face. "You are the best thing to ever happen to me.

You helped me find happiness again. You made me feel like I had a family for the first time. Chris, I love you so much it hurts."

"Then why did you keep me in the dark?" he whispered. "Why did I have to hear it from Steve and not my own wife?"

Lucy hiccupped. "Because I was ashamed of what I'd done. I had already barged into your life. The last thing I wanted was for you to find out I was a lying thief. I didn't want you to hate me. I didn't want to be a burden."

Christopher kissed her roughly, nearly bruising her lips as if he wanted to get one thing through her head. "Listen to me, Lucy Bennington you have never, ever been a nuisance to me. You are my adoring wife. My role is to love, cherish, and above all to protect you until death do us part. Is that clear?"

"Yes, Christopher," Lucy responded softly as she patted his cheek. "Crystal clear."

Chapter 17

----

1 MONTH LATER...

"Lucy, will you please tell me what's going on in that pretty head of yours? You've been looking at me with your beautiful sad eyes for weeks like a lamb waiting to be slaughtered." Christopher tucked away a brown curl over her ear as she arranged his bookshelf for the fifth time that month.

To say Lucy was feeling restless ever since Poppy injured Thatcher was an understatement. She'd been as nervous as a newborn chick and constantly fluttering all over the house cleaning things that didn't need to be cleaned and hiding her worries inside her head. The latter which had caused her a boatload of trouble already.

He knew Lucy wasn't worried about his family, they had been wonderfully understanding despite the fact Lucy had stolen their money and belongings—the money which had since been returned to them—and they had been nothing but kind to her during her ordeal. Though Christopher might have threatened them to keep their mouths shut.

Lucy hesitated before she avoided his eyes. "It's nothing."

"It's not nothing." Christopher tilted her chin toward him and forced her to stare at him. "You've been as nervous as a cat near a dog." She wrinkled her nose at the comparison which caused him to smile. At least she was reacting instead of acting like a statue.

He gripped her hand gently, sat down in his leather armchair and pulled her to sit on his lap. Christopher wrapped his arms around her, so she didn't squirm away. "Now, young lady, tell me what is it? Don't make me force it out of you. It won't be pretty."

Lucy hesitated. Her eyes shifted from her lap to her feet, and finally to him. The words which came out of her mouth were a surprise to say the least. "I want you to spank me."

He raised a dark eyebrow in surprise. "What? Why? You nearly fainted when I spanked you with the spoon months ago."

"I know." She started fidgeting in his lap causing his cock to stir in his trousers. "But Poppy got spanked because of me and it wasn't even her problem in the first place."

"Poppy got whipped because she likes to meddle and if it wasn't 1870, I would marry her off to Finn so the little hellion becomes his problem. He seems to be a glutton for punishment." His voice darkened. "So, is this why you asked for a spanking? You feel guilty because Poppy got spanked and you didn't?"

She nodded.

"Lu, I wasn't planning on spanking you. You know this. I already think the stress you went through with Thatcher was enough punishment."

Lucy bit her lip, obviously not agreeing with him.

Christopher sighed as he rocked her in his lap. Her hair was growing nicely, and the curly brown tresses nearly reached her shoulders. "Would a spanking make you feel better, Lu? Will it help the guilt to settle and put everything behind us so we can act like the normal married couple we were before this?"

"We hardly met under usual circumstances, Chris," she whispered. "I didn't really give you much choice when I showed up unannounced."

He chuckled as he kissed her temple. "At least we have a nice story to share with our grandchildren."

"Christopher, about the other thing," she shut her eyes tightly, "please spank me. It will make me feel better, I promise."

Christopher looked perplexed as he ran a hand through his dark hair, he looked like he was about to disagree, but when he saw how she was practically pleading for it he pointed to the staircase. "Go upstairs and remove every piece of clothing. I will be there shortly."

A blush crept over her cheeks as she nodded, and hurriedly made her way up to their bedroom where she removed her clothing. It felt weird standing naked and waiting, even if it was in their bedroom, considering they had made love constantly in here ever since they wed.

Though she supposed this time it was different because she was to be punished instead of being brought to pleasure. She squirmed, trying to cover her nudeness when her husband came in holding a long, thick switch. It had been cleaned off of any leaves or splinters and it had clearly been cut from the lemon tree in the backyard.

Lucy had never been switched before, but it couldn't hurt worse than the wooden spoon, could it?

"You're ready. Lovely." He pointed the switch towards the wooden chair he pulled from her vanity table. "Bend over Lucy, darling. All the way, that's a good girl. Your bottom should be dangling from the chair."

Her cheeks grew even redder, representing as two bright

red tomatoes. She felt like she was a fish dangling from a fishing pole with her bottom stuck in the air. Her legs parted slightly in her humiliating position, and she felt a gush of air hit her bare cunny.

Lucy stiffened when she felt Christopher softly rubbing the switch over her rear end as if preparing his target. "I'm going to give you twenty strokes. Let's hope we never have to repeat this lesson again."

Twenty strokes! She would never survive, though she was glad Chris was one of those husbands who told her how many strokes she was getting so she wasn't lying there wondering when the punishment was going to end.

"Are you ready, Lucy darling?"

"Y-Yes sir."

"Good girl."

The switch swished through the air before landing on her bare bottom creating a faint pink line in the center of both cheeks and delivering a cutting sting. Lucy yelped as the second and third switch landed on the same spot. Perhaps she was wrong, and a switching was much worse than being paddled with the wooden spoon.

The switch landed fast and hard, stroke after stroke, as Christopher blistered every inch of her bottom leaving no paleness behind. He wanted every part of her rear end to be a vivid scarlet hue to remind her what would happen if she chose to willingly keep something from him again.

"I am your husband," he scolded as he landed the switch extra hard twice on the sensitive spot where butt met thigh causing Lucy to burst into tears. "You do not keep secrets from me, is that understood, Lucy?"

"Yes sir!" Lucy cried out as she felt him deliver the spanking sternly as fresh tears poured down her cheeks.

Her ass felt like it was on fire. She continued holding on to the chair tightly as the switch continued to land. Her bouncing cheeks went from a dusty pink to a deep red, and were decorated quickly with swelling welts which, no doubt, would be itching tomorrow.

Lucy was dreading sitting for the next few days. It was going to be torture. Her bottom felt hot, achy, and swollen as her cheeks jiggled lewdly from the power of the switch. She would never be able to see the lemon tree through the same eyes again. To her it would always be the tree her husband cut a switch from for the first time.

"Are you going to be my very good girl from now on, Lu?"

Lucy groaned as he put away the switch, and then squeezed both butt cheeks in each hand roughly. His hands massaged the blistered nates and his fingers rubbed on the welts as an extra punishment.

"I'll be good, Chris. I swear." She tried to wiggle away from his large hands, but it was nearly impossible while he gripped her aching cheeks.

He finally cut short his torture and removed his hands from her bottom cheeks. Christopher helped her stand, then started kissing the tears away. "There's my good girl."

Lucy felt a salty tear land on her tongue as she enjoyed his soft, sweet kiss. She didn't know how to explain it, but after being thoroughly punished she felt lighter, and her heart didn't feel as heavy as it had in the beginning.

Christopher's hand started lowering toward her mound which caused her to feel a familiar throbbing between her legs. Even though her ass burned and was covered in welts, she couldn't deny the moisture of her desire which had gathered during her punishment, which no doubt her husband had noticed, too.

His fingers, at first, ran through the chocolate brown curls before he started rubbing her swollen little clit which had started peeking from its hood. "Aren't we a little wet?" he chuckled in her ear causing her to blush for an entirely different reason. He jabbed a finger inside of her. "Or should I say soaking?"

"Don't tease me," she begged as his quick fingers started rubbing her clit which was nearly dark red with need. It was like she wanted Christopher's fingers on her clit, but she was feeling shy about the teasing at the same time.

"Don't pull away from me, sweetheart," he warned as he alternated between spreading her love lips open and rubbing them with his large paw to make them as equally swollen as every part of her. "Do you want me to bury myself inside your sweet little cunny? You're ready for me, aren't you?"

She thrust her hips in response, bitterly disappointed she didn't have something inside her. That something in specific being her husband's cock. "Yes," she managed to say as her nipples puckered. This caught Christopher's attention as he started to gently bite them, his teeth scraping her sensitive flesh until she shivered.

"Say that you want me, Lucy." He started nibbling on the shell of her ear which only caused her to rub her body against him even more.

"I want you, Christopher." Her lower lip trembled with almost quiet desperation. "Please make love to me."

Christopher discarded his clothes with the same need she had for him. "Wrap your arms around my neck," he instructed hoarsely.

His erection was throbbing against her lower belly: a reddish, angry purple member with thick veins surrounding it which nearly jumped whenever it saw Lucy.

Lucy did as she was told as Christopher held her by her waist so she could wrap her legs around his torso. While her wet, aching pussy rubbed against the hard muscles of his stomach she felt his manhood rub against the bottom of her punished cheeks.

A whimper escaped her lips as he squeezed her sore nates firmly in his hands as he carried her back to their bed. He placed her down gently before he positioned himself at her center, gripping the back of each thigh.

Lucy felt empty and needy, she didn't even care that her freshly spanked ass was digging against the mattress. She just wanted her husband to satisfy her before she went insane. It didn't help that he was rubbing her thighs slowly causing the growing need to settle in her core.

Christopher thrust inside her in one quick push, her pooling wetness causing her to adjust to him easily. His movements were unexpected but welcomed according to Lucy who had started fondling her breasts as her husband buried himself inside her.

Christopher's cock stretched her small opening as he inched himself forward until every part of him was buried in her tight quim. He gripped her thighs feeling the welts he had put there with his own switch. Her sweet moans made him grow hotter and her cunny to drip even more with her wetness at the prospect of being properly punished and then fucked.

"Touch yourself between your legs," he grunted as he adjusted himself with her legs nearly resting on his shoulders.

Lucy quickly followed orders as she started rubbing herself with the pads of her fingers feeling her clit pulse as her husband started fucking her in slow, rigid strokes.

The rubbing of her clit matched his thrusts each time he withdrew himself from her, only to pierce her with his manhood again. Their bodies entwined with each other's as Lucy's breasts bounced against the rhythm of his hips and his muscular thighs hit her sore rear end. Lucy felt like every part of her was bursting with sensation, like she was on fire, and it was all caused by her husband and the way he handled her body with both roughness and gentleness.

Lucy's moans were ringing deliciously in his ear despite the fact her sore bottom was rubbing continuously against the bedspread. "Oh, oh Chris! That feels wonderful. Oh, I love you."

Christopher finished inside her, feeling as his warm seed seeped out of her womanhood. He started landing kisses down her neck and toward her mound which was covered with the remnants of his come. "Not as much as I love you, Lucy Bennington."

<hr>

Chapter 18

<hr>

"Happy Birthday, Lucy!"

Lucy Bennington grinned widely as she looked at the large cake with buttercream frosting and lilac roses made from sweet icing. Her sisters-in-law had organized a surprise party while her husband kept her occupied in their bed.

Apparently, Iris had quite a talent for decorating cakes, so she had taken care of the baking. Lily had decorated the table with paper hearts and crowns made out of cardboard. Poppy had bullied Hugh into helping decorate the Benningtons' second home with balloons and paper streamers.

When Lucy had stepped into the house under the pretense of being invited to dinner her eyes watered with tears. They had come so far in just a year, after a rather rocky start the Benningtons had finally accepted her as one of their own. Even though her dear husband would have argued she had won their hearts months ago.

She rubbed her wedding ring as she looked at the long

table while Christopher squeezed her shoulder. Lucy felt happy, she felt loved. She had finally received the wish she had prayed for since she was a small child: a family.

Her eyes shone with tears as she looked around the Bennington family. Lily was looking at her with adoring eyes while the crown she was wearing went lopsided. Iris was cutting the birthday cake into perfect slices while Anthony arranged the presents next to her so she could easily open them.

Hugh was discreetly lighting a cigar and he winked at her when he noticed her staring. Poppy looked gleeful and happy; Lucy knew it was because she had recently started courting a new beau. Lucy couldn't help but notice that Finn looked at Poppy with a mix of pain and adoration, still clearly in love with her. Poppy was avoiding looking at him entirely. The two of them were still doing a weird mating ritual. Even though Poppy and Finn were at each other's throats the majority of the time, she couldn't help but think of Finn as family as well. He had become almost an older brother figure to Lucy.

Steve was standing behind Finn and he looked different. Lucy couldn't quite put her mind to what it was, but he looked troubled, which was something someone as carefree as Steve Bennington rarely was. She wondered if there was something going on in town, but Larkspur Valley has been relatively quiet since Thatcher's sentencing.

Steve was smiling at her, but it didn't quite reach his eyes. Out of all the Bennington siblings he had always been the jokester, but right now he looked downright miserable as if he were preparing for his own funeral. He looked like a caged animal, Lucy was about to inquire what was wrong, but he turned around and headed outside.

"Here, sweetheart." Christopher was holding some cake

on a fork trying to feed her. Lucy opened her mouth, her tongue caressing the extra frosting on her bottom lip.

Iris turned away in secondhand embarrassment. She was sixteen, but still got easily flushed when it came to matters of love much like Lucy had been. Christopher had told her she was of age to court now if she wanted to, but the young man had to meet them first. Iris had waved them off by saying she wouldn't torture any man by having him meet her brothers and that she had no interest in courting. Lucy had a sneaking suspicion Iris's brothers were trying to marry her off in the next two years so they could avoid arguing with her about her insistence on working for a living. She faced Poppy and asked, "Is Richard coming?"

Richard Glass was Poppy's latest beau, he was the same age as she, and worked at the post office. They had started courting when Poppy had sent out a letter to a friend who had moved to New York. Lucy had never seen her so happy, and she told her siblings that Richard was the man she would marry, but every once in a while she noticed Poppy looking at Finn, especially during church which made her want to shake her for being so stubborn.

It was obvious Finn felt love for Poppy and would gladly whisk her away to the nearest church if she agreed to marry him. Poppy, on the other hand, complained she hated being spanked and treated like a little girl by Finn, and that once she married Richard, Finn could never butt into her business again.

Poppy nodded as she fiddled with her cake. "He gets off at six-thirty. He should be here soon, I helped him pick your present, Lucy."

Lucy forced a smile on her face giving Finn an apologetic look. Finn scowled at the blonde who had been his obsession for years and left without bothering to say goodbye.

Anthony cleared his throat, trying to hide the awkwardness. "I'll be delivering my sermon on Sunday. Will you come?" Anthony had graduated early from divinity school a few months ago and had taken over Larkspur Valley's Presbyterian Church when the old pastor decided to move back east to be closer to his extended family.

Hugh playfully put him in a chokehold. "Of course, we will, runt. Do you honestly think we'll miss you making a fool out of yourself?"

"Hugh don't be mean," Lily shrieked as she looked at Anthony with adoring eyes. "Anthony, will be a wonderful pastor."

While the rest of the Bennington siblings were distracted, Lucy whispered in Christopher's ear, "Go outside and check on Steve."

He frowned. "Why?"

"He seems upset. I think he needs someone to talk to. Go see what's wrong."

Christopher didn't seem convinced, but he nibbled on the shell of her ear before departing outside. Women seemed to think everything was resolved by talking while men knew they just needed some peace and quiet to clear their thoughts and make some hard decisions.

The oldest Bennington sibling headed outside and found Steve punching a stray haystack, a pained look on his face. His knuckles were blistered and covered with blood which meant Hugh would have to take a look at them. Christopher raised an eyebrow. "What did that haystack do to you?"

Steve gave him a sour expression. "What are you doing here?"

"Lucy sent me. She's worried about you."

"She doesn't have to be." He punched the haystack again.

Christopher pulled him away, pushing him against the haystack so he couldn't hurt himself anymore. He gripped him by the shoulder. "What's wrong? I cannot help you if you don't tell me."

Steve laughed humorlessly. "Can you take care of a pregnancy?"

Christopher pulled back. "Pregnancy? Who's pregnant?"

Steve didn't say anything for a few minutes, but he had a somber expression on his face. "Ruby."

"Ruby?" Christopher frowned. "I didn't know you were courting anyone."

"I'm not," he said tightly. "Ruby is a fallen woman. She works at Madam Eugenia's whorehouse. I've been going to her for a few months. She's only nineteen." He shut his eyes. "She's three months pregnant, the only reason the little chit finally squealed was because she was attempting to get rid of the baby."

"Would that have been so bad?" Christopher asked lightly. "She's a soiled dove. You two will never be able to live peacefully in Larkspur Valley, perhaps it would be best—"

Steve's eyes became murderous as he pushed his brother. "Would you tell Lucy the same thing?"

"Of course not, but she's not pregnant. Besides we're married," Christopher stated calmly. "You got this Ruby pregnant out of wedlock and she's a fallen woman."

"Stop calling her that," Steve hissed at him.

"You know I'm right, neither you nor Ruby or the baby will have a happy life if she gives birth to the baby," Christopher announced calmly. "You should have been more careful. The way I see it you have three options: first, you send Ruby away from Larkspur Valley so she has a chance at a decent life, second, she gets rid of the baby and there are medicine women who can help with that option and it's where Ruby seems to be headed, or third, you do the decent thing and marry the girl. The rumors and dirty looks will die off eventually; you should be man enough to take it."

Steve ran a hand through his dark hair, sulking. "She doesn't want to get married. I already proposed. She wants to get rid of the baby and continue bedding strangers for a living."

Christopher took a deep breath, torn between wanting to comfort his brother and strangle him for being so stupid as to get a girl pregnant. "Is there anything I can do to help?"

Steve shook his head sadly. "No, I will take care of it. Go back and enjoy your wife's birthday. Give Lucy my apologies. I'm going to the saloon to get myself a much-needed drink."

"Steve, what kind of girl is Ruby?"

He shook his head. "A stubborn, arrogant, little hellion who would argue with God if He stood before her. She can be sweet when she wants to be, which is rare. She's kind of like a cactus."

Christopher snorted. "Lucky man. I'll see you tomorrow."

Christopher was still lost in his own thoughts when he reentered the house. Anthony and Hugh were talking with Poppy's new beau, Richard, while the girls cleaned up. He rested his hands on Lucy's hips and silently ordered her to come with him.

Lucy followed her husband to his old study which Iris had transformed into a little library. She sat down in a pastel blue chair and placed her hands on her lap. "Is everything all right with Steve? I've never seen him so unhappy."

"He got someone pregnant," Christopher said calmly, there was no point in beating around the bush. "A soiled dove from the town brothel. A girl named Ruby. She's a pretty, young thing according to Steve. She's a little older than Iris. Nineteen, I think. She's three months pregnant."

Lucy gaped and stood up. It was one shock after the other. "What is he going to do? How can I help?"

"It is Steve's business, he doesn't want us involved,

darlin'." Christopher wrapped his arms around her pulling her close. She could feel his erection pressing against her lower belly. "Did you enjoy your birthday?"

She nodded as she buried her face in his chest. "Very much. All of you planned a wonderful surprise. Thank you." Lucy pulled back. "You haven't given me my present."

"What do you mean? I gave you those beautiful silver combs with the amethyst stones." He ran a hand through her curly brown hair which now reached her shoulders. "What else do you want, Mrs. Bennington?"

A coy smile appeared on her lips as she got on her tippy toes. "A kiss."

Christopher laughed as he engulfed her in a deep, passionate kiss. He wrapped his arms around her waist and spun her around like a rag doll. He chuckled, kissing the tip of her nose. "Happy birthday, my darling wife."

Annabelle Marin

Annabelle Marin is a twenty-something romantic who lives in sunny California. When she isn't writing she enjoys daydreaming, watching way too much TV, and cuddling with her pets.

Her books are sweet erotic romances with domestic discipline. In her books you can expect: a spoonful of sweetness, a dash of sass, a cup of naughtiness, and an abundance of romance.

You can follow Annabelle on Facebook, Instagram, Goodreads, and Bookbub for exciting updates on upcoming books!

Facebook-https://www.facebook.com/annabelle.marin.940/
Instagram-https://www.instagram.com/
missannabellemarin/
Bookbub-//www.bookbub.com/profile/annabelle-marin
Goodreads-www.goodreads.com/author/show/21061973.
Annabelle_Marin

Don't miss these exciting titles by Annabelle Marin and Blushing Books!

Endless Paradise
Between Kisses & Lies
Letters to Holly

The Hollis Sisters

The Affair
The Scandal

The Stevenson Brothers Series
The Rancher Orders a Bride
The Pastor Takes a Wife
The Sheriff Finds a Fiancée

Vintage Beauties Series
Bless Her Heart
Becoming a Gibson Girl

The Bride Series
The Unwilling Mrs.
The Unattainable Bride
The Unexpected Wife

Anthologies
12 Naughty Days of Christmas 2021

Blushing Books

Blushing Books is one of the oldest eBook publishers on the web. We've been running websites that publish spanking and BDSM related romance and erotica since 1999, and we have been selling eBooks since 2003. We hope you'll check out our hundreds of offerings at http://www.blushingbooks.com.

Blushing Books Newsletter

Please join the Blushing Books newsletter
to receive updates & special promotional offers.
You can also join by using your mobile phone:
Just text **BLUSHING** to 22828.